What readers say about Harlequin Romances

"Harlequins take away the world's troubles and for a while you can live in a world of your own where love reigns supreme."
L.S.,* Beltsville, Maryland

"Thank you for bringing romance back to me."
J.W., Tehachapi, California

"I find Harlequins are the only stories on the market that give me a satisfying romance with sufficient depth without being maudlin."
C.S., Bangor, Maine

"Harlequins are magic carpets...away from pain and depression...away to other people and other countries one might never know otherwise."
H.R., Akron, Ohio

*Names available on request

OTHER
Harlequin Romances
by JOYCE DINGWELL

Deep in the Forest

by

JOYCE DINGWELL

Harlequin Books

TORONTO • LONDON • NEW YORK • AMSTERDAM • SYDNEY

Original hardcover edition published in 1975
by Mills & Boon Limited

ISBN 0-373-01961-0

Harlequin edition published April 1976

Second printing November 1977

PRINTED IN U.S.A.

CHAPTER ONE

THE jinker-flattened track from the valley often dodged large trees, sometimes crossed singing streams, occasionally stumbled over huge clinkers, but always wound *up*. Up, beneath a leafy roof that shut out the sky, up past unwanted logs mouldering into rich chocolate earth, up to the ledge, and the boss's house beneath the ledge, at the peak.

But before the track reached Tall Tops, and the woodmen's chalets around Tall Tops, it passed the garages, petrol pumps, tool depositories and the mill. The power for the mill came from waste wood that fed giant boilers, and the purpose of the mill was to deal swiftly and accurately with hundreds of feet of once-proud forest. The process never failed to sadden Selina, since she loved the trees, but the mountains of resultant sawdust always brightened her again. Twenty tons were added to it daily, and each load took on a different gradation of gold. At least, Selina thought, some of the forest beauty was won back.

Selina was always cheered, too, by the friendly waves from the chalets, from the bachelor woodsmen hoping to get a dance at the next ledge 'hop', from the children whose correspondence lessons she supervised and from their anxious mothers who hoped to keep it like that.

The last chalet, more villa in size than chalet as befitted the overseer, particularly sent her spirits soaring. She had been attracted to Roger Peters from the moment he had arrived here from the Forestry Academy. She felt he was attracted to her.

Snatching at a bar of song now, she turned the bend of the timber track . . . and her spirits zeroed.

Him.

'Him' in this instance was Joel Grant from Redgum Ridge, another large timber holding as was Tall Tops, but although Grant was affluent now, the big, rather Red Indian-looking man had come up the hard way, felling yellow box or ironbark for railway sleepers for years to set himself up to stock his large parcel of mountain, and now his past persisted. He was either Iron or Ironbark to everyone. What . . . and Selina whisked away a giggle . . . if he had been tagged Yellow Box instead?

"The lady seems amused." Iron Grant, who had evidently been visiting Tall Tops, was poking at his pipe with a twig and waiting for her to join him. She did not want to join him, but she supposed for politeness' sake she must. Besides, there was nowhere else to go.

The man was not young . . . she had reached him by now . . . yet on the other hand he was not old. You couldn't be certain about his age, in fact the only thing you could be certain about Iron Grant was that he was tough.

"No cedar, no maple about him," Roger had remarked demeaningly . . . Roger had introduced finer, more selective timber to Tall Tops . . . "only stuff for mine props, ceiling joists—"

"Railway sleepers," Selina had finished. They had both laughed scornfully, though Selina had been care-

6

ful with her laughter. She was, and always had been, a little nervous with Iron Grant. However, it was too late now to hide today's laughter.

"Yes, I am amused," she agreed perfunctorily.

"Can I share the joke?"

"It was only something one of my children said." She knew he would know she meant one of her correspondence charges.

"It's Saturday. They're not at lessons today, they're round at the pool. I've been supervising them."

"Good of you."

"Seeing I donated the pool" ... he said it quite naturally but, disliking him, Selina branded him boastful ... "I thought I should. I, too, like children. We two should think over that mutual liking one day." A deliberate pause. "Do something about it."

She turned away in disgust. Really, Roger could not have said a truer thing, the man most certainly was not, and never would be, cedar.

"No, only ironbark." He must have read her thoughts.

"My choice was yellow box." She slipped past him and ran up the path to Tall Tops. As she went through the open door and down the long hall she heard his car, that big, imported, very expensive car simply reeking of prosperity that Roger, poor dear, bitterly envied, going along his private road to Redgum Ridge.

Tall Tops was a comfortable old house with nooks and ingles and verandahs and annexes simply everywhere. When Selina had first seen it she had thought it must be the biggest house in the world. Now she knew better. She knew by going there *once*, since

Uncle Claud had insisted she drive him over, that Redgum Ridge was bigger and better, richer. There must be money in sleepers, joists and props, she had reported contemptuously to Roger, for she would not have dared to say it to Uncle Claud. He liked the fellow.

"Of course," Roger had patronised in return.

Dear Roger, Roger of the academic learning, not the learning that comes from an axe felling hardwood, it wasn't fair that Roger didn't have the Grant money instead. However . . . a fond little smile . . . money meant nothing, not when you—when both of you— She called : "Are you there, Unk?" and began peeping in each of the rooms in turn.

Unk was not really Uncle, nor any relation at all. When Selina had first gasped at the size of Tall Tops she had stood beside her elder sister and her mother, and Mrs. Lockwood, her mother, had come to house-keep for Mr. Whittier, now Unk.

The old bachelor, old even then, Selina remembered, so how old must Unk be now, had smiled and won them over at once—well, won Mrs. Lockwood and Selina. Madeleine, eleven to Selina's seven, had stood aloof.

Madeleine had persisted in her aloofness, and at last in despair Mr. Whittier, who liked having happy people around him, had asked Madeleine would she like to go to a boarding school in Sydney.

Madeleine, having made certain *which* school, had liked the idea very much, and from then on they had only seen her during vacations, and, as she grew older, not even then, since she preferred to stay at the friends' homes rather than go bush. Mrs. Lockwood had not worried; perhaps already she had re-cognised in Madeleine some of the traits she had known in her husband whom she had not heard of for years. As for Selina, she had not cared at all. She and Madeleine had never been close. Selina's only concern had been that one day she might wake up and find this wonderful world of trees, of ferns and wild orchids, of twilight jungles, of singing birds and singing streams . . . yes, and gold-layered sawdust . . . was all a dream.

But the dream had lasted. School for Selina, the same as school for the children in the chalets, had come through the post, and later when her mother had died life had gone on just the same, except for a dear one missing, for the girl and the old man. For old Uncle Claud.

"Claud, where are you?" Selina called in exaspera-tion now. She always dropped niceties when she was running out of patience.

"Uncle from saplings." Claud Whittier came out from behind a paper. "Who do you think you are, young 'un?"

"Not as young as you're thinking, and definitely not a sapling any more. I see you've had Ironbark for tea."

"Joel's the name, and the tea was beer."

"Beer certainly sounds more like him." Roger had a wonderful knowledge of wines, and he had even built a special cellar. "What did he want?"

"You have it the wrong way round. I wanted him."

"What for?"

"Nosey!"

"Sorry, Unk, but what should he know that I

9

shouldn't?"

"Well, what's in my will, for one thing." The old man said it jocundly, but had Selina looked across at him she would have seen the hard look he gave her.

"You and your old will!" she dismissed. "You'll live for years yet, probably be choked off in the end by parasitic fig."

"Just so long as I fall in the wind and am not sawn or axed." Uncle added feelingly: "Or milled."

"You'll grow fungus as a grounded log."

"But orchids, too."

"Darling, I promise I'll plant orchids all over you. Chops or steak?" Here in the mountain where there were no stores, provisions had to be bought in bulk and then deep frozen.

"Surprise me," said Uncle Claud, and took up his paper again.

Selina went out to the country kitchen. Although Claud Whittier had allowed Selina's mother a free hand, and a generous hand, with everything, Mrs. Lockwood had preferred to keep the old house as she had found it, and particularly the kitchen. Mostly brown, raftered, cool even when big dinners were roasting, the white plates and cups, clean-gleaming in the colonial dresser, still winked a welcome every time Selina entered. It was one of those kitchens, she had always thought fancifully, from which the smell of gingerbread should steal. She had tried it out once on Roger, but he didn't like gingerbread. His preference for the four o'clock repast was wafer bread and butter and lemon tea. Roger had impeccable taste.

She decided on chops for tonight, removed them from the freezer and took the hoary parcel to the window to start to thaw. As usual she looked out of the window, looked out and caught her breath. Will I ever, she thought with sweet pain, look out of Tall Tops' windows and not catch my breath?

The location was New South Wales, yet so close to the Queensland border that Uncle Claud often declared that most of his trees had their leaves in Queensland even though their roots were in the southern state. The climate was perfect for timber; there was the refreshing cool that comes with high places to suit the colder weather trees, but the sub-tropical lushness to encourage the more flamboyant specimens. Also . . . and another catch in Selina's breath . . . there were wild limes, wild orchids, trees that looked as though they were spattered with paint until you peered closer and saw that they were alive with rainbow parrots, there were lichens, unbelievable mosses, trails of old man's beard.

Then there were the encroaching trees, not the disciplined ones for future milling, but the individuals that Uncle allowed to climb up the valley almost to Tall Tops' door. She knew them all now, and loved them all, blackwoods, sassafras, ash, walnut, silky oak, mahogany. One, a favourite 'boy', was a two-hundred-foot grey gum.

"Too big for his boots," Unk always said, but he wouldn't allow him to be lopped. The grey was the child of an outcast from a white gum community a mile south. That sometimes happened in the eucalypt world. A ghetto of gum would resist the intrusion of a different variety of gum. This particular white gum valley must be one of the most beautiful valleys, Selina thought, in the world. Every tree trunk in it

11

was, and had been, snow white as though whitewashed that way . . . until, some years ago, there was one grey intruder. The intruder had eventually perished, even an experienced forester could not have explained how or why, but not before seed had been sown, and another small tree begun its cycle. But safely away this time from the white gum ghetto . . . Uncle had seen to that . . . and just to show them all the new grey had soared higher than the whites ever had aspired.

"You may not be as beautiful," Uncle had said to the tree, "but I'll say this, you're gutsy."

They called the grey The Big Feller.

Selina looked beyond the grey gum to distant Redgum Ridge. *His* place. He was higher than Tall Tops, in fact his forest was the highest on all the ledge. She first had met 'him' when she had gone down with Unk to the tree nursery, which was tucked away safely in a sheltered valley near the boundary fence. The new man, Joel Grant, had been attending to his side of the fence. He had come forward at once and put his hand out to Unk, and Unk had grasped it.

"Name of Grant—Joel Grant. I've taken over Redgum Ridge."

"You chose well. I'm Claud Whittier of Tall Tops. This here is my most promising sapling." Uncle had brought Selina forward.

"Yes," Joel Grant had agreed, "pushing up nicely." It hadn't been his words that had affronted Selina, though she hadn't cared much for them, either, it had been his eyes, bantering but unrevealing eyes, eyes that never moved from your face, yet eyes you still were sharply aware hadn't missed one indignant inch. How different, she had thought, from their new overseer, who had arrived that same week. Roger Peters had stepped forward, taken her hand, then with a little soft laugh to cover any embarrassment over the lovely old world courtesy, kissed it.

Roger. She turned her glance from the highest point on the ledge, from Redgum Ridge, and looked down to the overseer's quarters instead. What a wonderful difference Roger had made to Carmody's house. When old Pat Carmody, the previous overseer, had retired, the house had been the same as when Pat had gone into it, fifteen years ago—brown, spare, very male.

It was male still, but elegantly male. Roger had wonderful perception. Some might think that the colours Roger chose did not suit the forest scene, but, as Roger pointed out, when it came to interiors the scene outside should take second place to the setting inside, not vice versa.

"You should have been a decorator, Roger," Selina had told him in admiration.

"Perhaps, but the real money was here. I saw that at once."

That was another thing about Roger, he had a good head for finance. Already he had almost doubled the planting in the nursery, and though Unk was not entirely in favour, he had to admit it could be profitable.

"Which *counts*, sir." Roger always called Uncle Claud sir.

"Maybe, but I like my boys to have plenty of room."

"There is sufficient space, I assure you. Don't forget, sir, I've studied the theory side, I've graduated in it."

13

"I'm not forgetting, young Peters." (Roger had stiffened at that, and Selina had not blamed him; she really should speak to Unk.) "But they're not just mill lengths, remember."

Roger had smiled pleasantly and placatingly. That was one of the things she loved about him, he was always courteous, always perfectly polite and solicitous, always deferential to status such as Unk's status as boss. *One* of the things? she smiled now to herself. No, one of the *many* things.

She saw Roger come to the front porch of his bungalow and look up to Tall Tops. He must be finished for the day. She placed the chops in a good thawing position, and went out of the back door and across to the overseer's villa. It was only some fifty yards away.

Roger opened his door before she could knock. He must have seen her coming. He smiled and bowed her in, and she entered and looked around with fresh appreciation on all the tasteful things with which the overseer had surrounded himself.

"Roger, it *is* nice."

"It's nicer now you're here." He plumped a cushion for her and seated her. "What did you do with yourself today?"

"No school as it's Saturday, so I went down the valley. I thought you might be there."

"At the cutting?" His lip curled. Most of the trees were mechanically sawn, but the hard-to-get timber was axe-cut. Selina felt she understood his sensitive distaste.

"I know," she soothed, "all those tree years trying to reach the sky, then suddenly, irrevocably, earthbound."

"Actually, Selina, it's the dust. It flies everywhere."

"Practical Roger!" She said it proudly. She admired Roger's clear thinking. If only Roger had had *someone else's* luck . . . she ignored years of hard grind . . . he would have made a fortune. Not that she wanted him to have a fortune, but he still would have, he had that capability. Thinking of Iron Grant made her mention the man now.

"*He* was visiting Unk when I got back," she said. "Ironbark Grant, Roger."

"Very interesting," Roger smiled teasingly, but a nice tease, not like the enigmatical Grant banter. "Was he visiting Mr. Whittier . . . or you?"

"Me?" she echoed.

"That's what I said, Selina."

A little formally she answered : "I told you, Roger, I came back and he was there. He was just leaving."

"Mission unsuccessful unless you were there?"

"Oh, Roger, you fool!"

"I'm not a fool, Sellie. The man's male, quite aggressively male I'd say, and you're the only eligible female for miles. Not only eligible but lovely, yes, lovely, and" . . . a pause . . . "promising."

"Promising?" she queried.

"Promising rich rewards. Oh, come, Sellie, your uncle is sitting very pretty, and you've told me he has no one of his own."

"No, but you're still very wrong, Roger. Unk has his trees, yes, but Tall Tops is on Crown land. All the land up here is Commonwealth-owned, Commonwealth-leased."

"But able to be altered now to private ownership.

15

Yes, Selina, that's true. Under our present government the land can be purchased at a nominal rate after certain requirements have been fulfilled. So you see you could attract our ironbark friend after all."

Selina was silent for a few moments; she did not like the turn that the conversation had taken. Roger must have sensed her distaste, for at once he crossed to her, sat down beside her and took both her hands in his.

"Little Sellie," he said softly, "darling little Sellie." And then he wasn't just holding her hands with his hands any more, he was holding her face between his hands instead, soft, very well-tended hands for a forester. He was kissing her. Reaching eagerly up, Selina was kissing him back. It was their initial caress.

That first kiss was all that it should be, Selina felt, it was dew and wonder and standing on tiptoe. Rainbows. There's a shining, she thought.

She got to her feet, then turned and left the house, glad when Roger did not stop her. It meant he felt the tallness of the moment, too. She ran across to the homestead, and saw yet didn't really see that the chops had defrosted. She should put them on . . . start dinner . . . but instead she went into the living room where Unk was still buried in papers.

She knew if she spoke, she would blurt, so it would be better to keep silent until she could contain herself. Yet she couldn't . . . *she couldn't*. Anyway, why try to keep it from Uncle when the glow must be showing? She felt she would shine in the darkest room, shine even down in the twilight jungle where the sun never reached and it was perpetual elf night.

"Uncle Claud." Yes, it was a blurt.

16

He must have noticed the change in her voice, for he lowered the paper and looked over it. "Yes, Sapling?" he asked.

"Love," she said breathlessly.

Then she said: "Roger. Me. Both of us. Uncle Claud, we love each other."

CHAPTER TWO

SELINA had not expected excitement or joy from Uncle Claud, after all he was an old man and his first reaction naturally would be surprise, even slight shock, but on the other hand she certainly had not anticipated dismay. Yes, dismay.

"You *what*?" Uncle echoed.

"We—we're in love." Selina felt she sounded a little silly the second time and was mildly embarrassed.

"That's more like it. There's a big difference in being in love and loving each other."

"To us," Selina said proudly, recovering her pride, "it's identical."

"You and the overseer?"

"Roger."

"I know his name. I should—I signed him on."

"And have been very satisfied since, Uncle."

"He's done his work," Unk admitted. "But then so did Pat Carmody."

"In a now superseded way. You have to go with the times, Uncle Claud. It's Roger's turn." A pause. "And mine."

"But," came in Mr. Whittier, "does it have to be together?"

"Yes," answered Selina, getting angry now. "I love Roger, Roger loves me."

". . . Or what comes with you?"

"Oh, not you now! Anyone would think I was

18

going to be an heiress. I'm well aware that this is only leasehold" ... Selina spread her hands to encompass what lay beyond the window ... "and that only the trees belong."

Just as Roger had said, Uncle Claud said: "Not now. Not any longer."

"Well, it's unimportant just the same, the important thing is—"

"That it's past six and no tucker." Uncle put up a barrage of newspaper, a barrage that somehow Selina could not find the courage to storm. She waited uncertainly a moment, then went back to the kitchen —where she promptly burned the chops and boiled the potatoes dry.

Not ... later ... that it mattered. Uncle Claud only picked at the meal. He always had a good appetite, and Selina decided he must be sulking. She put down her own knife and fork and looked sternly at the old man.

"You've always been one for nature, Unk, and this ... this lovely happening between Roger and me ... is nature. It's the greening, darling, it's the first stirring in the earth, it's—"

"It's kibosh," Uncle snapped.

"You're being unfair, terribly unfair to poor Roger. You've nothing against him."

"He plants too close."

"More profitable."

"Profit! *Profit!* Have I brought you up to count profit?"

"He—Roger was only thinking of you when he planted closer, and he does have academic backing."

"Academic hoo-ha! Another thing, or things. Two of them. His hands are soft—manicured."

"And why not?" Selina's temper was right up again. "Does he have to be Red Indian and cut his nails square to rate anything in your opinion?"

"Never wielded a saw, I'd hazard," continued Uncle Claud, ignoring Selina, "mechanical or manual. As for axes, he wouldn't know a spotted gum handle from a hickory."

"Of course he would, you have to admit he knows his timbers."

Grumpily Uncle conceded this, but he still could not bring himself to bless Selina . . . well, not bless perhaps, she wasn't expecting that, but at least not dash her down so completely. She took up her knife and fork again, but it was no good, she had no appetite. Neither had Unk. Anyway, looking at the burnt offering, it was a very poor meal. She took the remains to the Brents' piggery along the track, then came slowly back. It seemed impossible that one hour ago she had been walking on air.

She stood a long time by the window that night. Birdsong had ceased, but somewhere in the far bush she could hear the howl of a dingo. It would be safe for the dog to cry out to his mate now, for the mountains would lie as dark as the bloom on black grapes. Is my mate calling for me? she thought fancifully, and was annoyed at a slightly hysterical giggle somewhere in her. For dear Roger, she knew, simply wasn't that howling type. But he's the type I *want*, she told herself. He's the one I *love*. She became aware that unconsciously she had turned the direction of her glance to Redgum Ridge, only discernible now by one steady light. She was irritated that she was declaring silent things to Iron Grant, and not, as she had intended, to Uncle Claud.

Morning made everything different, for you could not wake up to a timber morning and not inherit the earth. The coachwhip birds made the first ringing sound, but they were promptly followed by the bell-birds' tink-tink. Soon afterwards the machine music of the sawmill joined the dawn orchestra, but not raspy at this distance, the rawness changed instead to rhythm. Through her window Selina could see Roger coming up to Tall Tops to discuss the day's doings with Uncle Claud as he always did. As ever he was wonderfully co-ordinated clothes-wise. Today it was rust corduroy pants, chamois-coloured shirt and desert boots. He looked faultless, and she knew his report on yesterday, which he would also give, would be fault-less, too. After Pat's garble, Uncle simply had to be impressed. She had shocked Uncle yesterday, but he would be reconciled now. Everything would be different.

She dressed hurriedly after wasting a few precious minutes choosing between jeans and shift. She wished she could be co-ordinated like Roger, but perhaps it would rub off him. By the time she reached the veran-dah Uncle and Roger were in deep discussion, and she saw that everything was all right, Uncle a little paler than usual, but quite composed again. He smiled at Selina, then asked Roger to stop for a bite. Roger looked at his watch and dutifully declined. Always the perfect employee, Selina glowed.

Over breakfast for two later, Uncle told Selina that today Roger and Joel Grant were going to make an initial survey for the extension of Grant's own small railway system into Tall Tops' forest.

"Joel has very generously offered to let us hook up on his line," Uncle said.

Selina already knew about this proposal through Roger. The train was one of the few things the overseer approved about Redgum Ridge.

"A bullock team in this year of grace," he had despaired of Tall Tops . . . there was only one team and it was kept for the hardest spots and out of sentiment the rest of the haulage was mechanised . . . "it has to be semi-trailers at least, or better still what *he* has fixed for himself. A train."

"Yes," said Selina unenthusiastically to Uncle now. Anything that man does, anything Iron Grant offers, must have a catch somewhere, she was thinking.

But after she had tidied the house, very little dusting here since the waste from the mill settled before it reached the top, she changed to jodphurs and boots and went down the track. As it was Sunday, the chalet children were having their Bible Lessons of the Air before they took off for the pool that Iron Grant had built for everyone's use. It was Mrs. Marlow's turn to supervise, and she waved to Selina. Selina waved back, and continued down the jinker-flattened road, hearing the mill music, the birds and the children singing *All Things Bright and Beautiful* and thinking fondly, as she had thought the first time she had listened, that timber silence was distinctly but wonderfully *loud*.

Within another minute it was even louder. There were voices raised. Selina went a few more steps, then stood behind a tree and listened. Then—cautiously— she looked.

Iron Grant and Roger were some yards from the

mill and they were facing each other.

"May I remind you," came Roger's clear concise voice, "that this has nothing at all to do with you. You are not on Ridge property now, Mr. Grant."

"I would damn well know that without you reminding me, do you think I would allow a hazard of this sort with kids around?"

What hazard? Selina wondered.

"The chalets," defended Roger, "are well away from the mill, and presumably the mothers—"

"A lot you know about youngsters, Peters! A mother can lock her child in a dungeon and he'll still get through the keyhole."

"You're being ridiculous."

"I'm being wise before an event."

"It's no business of yours," Roger reminded him again.

"A young 'un's life is everyone's business. Good lord, to let a heap accumulate like that!"

Now Selina knew what it was all about. It was the sawdust mountain, which, and she had to be honest about it, had grown much more lofty of late. But then it was difficult to stop it growing. It was hard to dispose of for the simple reason that no one wanted it. Every lumber camp had this problem, every lumber camp knew that if sawdust suddenly became valuable, they would be millionaires.

"The children are well aware of it," Roger was saying. "They are, after all, foresters' children."

"If you're using that argument the kids who come to my pool can swim, but I still watch them."

"I thought that would crop up sooner or later, that subject of your generosity."

"I'll let that pass...*this time*...Peters, there's something more important to thrash out now. If you don't do something about that pile, then I will—"

"Accepted gladly, Grant. Good of you to offer."

"Let me finish. *I will do something to you*."

"Oh, for heaven's sake, on to the barbarian stuff, are we? All right then, what do you suggest?"

"When you lay your line to meet mine I don't mind taking the waste away. I'm filling-in on the western side."

"I thought there was something else to all this."

"But until then"... Iron Grant's voice was iron as well... "close it in."

"Close it in?" Roger echoed angrily.

"Build a fence. And don't tell me you haven't enough timber."

"But you said yourself children will get through a keyhole."

"Then put barbed wire on top."

"Barbed wire!" Roger's voice was shocked, and Selina didn't wonder. Barbed wire!

"Affronts you, doesn't it? Well, it doesn't thrill me, either. But if I have to choose between that or a smothered youngster—"

The voices were dropping, the heat was going out of the argument. Presently Selina heard the steps receding down the valley. She looked at the retreating figures, both tall but one much broader. One perfectly dressed for his work and one— Well, Ironbark Grant would never be known for his taste in clothes.

Selina came out from behind the tree and went and looked at the sawdust mountain. She was sorry her golden pile was to be enclosed by a fence. She took up a stick and poked at it. After all, the children never even glanced at it. Foresters' children, as Roger had said, wouldn't bother. She pushed the stick in. She had done it a score of times before, and never started anything, but today she began an instant avalanche. A landslide of sawdust came rushing down at her . . . how had she ever admired the red-gold gradations? . . . and if she had not seen it coming and leapt smartly aside she would have been buried in the smothering waste. As it was, she was tumbled over in the sudden yellow flow, and the mound soared up almost to her hips. A child would have been knocked down. A child would have—choked.

Carefully extricating herself in case she started another landslide and this time completed the job of self-destruction, she edged and slithered and rolled away. Not till she reached the track did she dare stand up. She was filthy. She was absolutely covered in red-gold dust. She knew that her tow hair, a colour in hair that picks up grime like blotting paper picks up ink, would be a brilliant titian. She would have to sneak back to Tall Tops and bath and change at once. As she passed the Sunday School, the children's and Mrs. Marlow's heads reverently bowed, thank goodness, she thought of the earlier *All Things Bright and Beautiful*. She didn't think she'd ever consider sawdust bright and beautiful any more, and decidedly not in her hair.

As she tiptoed into the house she heard with relief Uncle's voice on the phone. Unk had an odd sense of humour (he called it a keen sense) and he would have laughed till he cried at her ruddy disarray and probably called: "Who's a Red Injun now?"

25

As it was she got safely to the bathroom without his hearing, or so she optimistically thought, but she did hear Uncle say into the phone:

"That's how I want it, Nossiter." Neil Nossiter of Tallow Wood, their nearest town, was Unk's solicitor. "Ring me back and let me know when it's ready for me to sign." What was there to sign, Selina thought without much interest, what's that old man up to now? She began shampooing madly.

The directions on the label of the shampoo had mentioned dust, grime, perspiration, dandruff, but, and not surprising, nothing about sawdust. The stuff stuck ... and stuck. Eventually she felt she could scrub and rinse no longer, and came out of the spray exhausted and waterlogged. More red wiped off again on to the towel, and the rest she decided to leave and hope it did not notice.

She changed into a dress, put on a fresh face and had just finished when she heard steps on the verandah and Uncle calling genially ... he would call genially to *him* ... for Joel Grant to come in.

She listened for Roger to be included, since he and Iron Grant had been together, but Roger wasn't mentioned, so he couldn't be there. So, she said mutinously, I needn't have bothered about my face after all. Not for *him*.

She stayed inside until Uncle shouted out for cuppas. He must have heard her in the shower, known she was in the house. She came out and put on the kettle. As she was jamming bread and butter she saw someone at the clothesline. She peered out of the window. Of all people it was Ironbark Grant. And of all things he was hanging up her jodhpurs!

26

"What on earth—" she began shouting furiously across to the line.

"I saw them on the bathroom floor—I was washing my hands after the valley. I know sawdust, and I can assure you if you don't get it all off at once you're stuck with it. So—" He waved magnaminously to the trews, pegged out in the uncomplimentary shape that jodhpurs do have until you are in them to shape them yourself.

She had so many things to say to him . . . *at* him . . . that she found she couldn't say any of them. Instead she heard herself inquiring coldly: "Do you make it a practice of looking on bathroom floors for soiled jodhpurs?"

"Not at all."

"Then—"

"But this time I expected them. You see, you left your exact print in the sawdust." He gave a significant pat to the seat of the wet pants.

"You—you—" Selina withdrew and angrily finished jamming the bread and butter, brewing the tea. She would have liked to have concluded the operation there, but Uncle would only call out to her if she didn't carry the thing to its bitter end. Bitter at this moment to her.

When she came out on the verandah the two men were deep in conversation. She distinctly heard ". . . any time you nominate" from Iron Grant to Uncle, and wondered what it was about. It must be about something, for Iron Grant cut it short when he saw her, and you only cut short things when they were important.

"I like your hair," he drawled. "A new rinse?"

Uncle grunted that he didn't know why women messed about with themselves. "The saplings's got hair the colour of peeled twigs, and that's a good shade," he said.

"Not peeled twigs now," said Iron Grant for Selina alone, "it has red-gold gradations. Almost sawdusty, one might say. Now about the join-up of your line, Claud, your overseer and I think—"

Selina poured the tea, put the cups beside the men, then escaped to the kitchen. As always she crossed to the window, and, seeing Roger at his window, she slipped out of the house and ran across to the villa.

Roger smiled a little wanly at her as he let her in.

"You've had a bad morning," she said sympathetically, seeing his despondency.

"Not a good one. That man—"

"Yes, he's a roughrider. Poor Roger." She noticed the direction of Roger's eyes, and put her hand up to her hair. "I fell in the sawdust. I've been washing it, and washing it, but it hasn't all come out."

At once he slipped his arms around her, and what he said was enough to make her love him even more —if she could love him more. It was so wonderful to meet a person so thoughtful, and, as it happened now, *honest* as Roger.

For—"Grant was right," Roger said ruefully. "I was wrong—that heap *is* dangerous. Oh, my Sellie, if you'd been hurt—"

The concern was too much for Selina. She put her head on his shoulder and suddenly cried. If anyone had told her she was crying because a man had laughed at her, had spanked the seat of her jodhpurs as he pinned them to a line, she would have looked at

28

them in horror. She was crying, she would have said, because Roger was so sweet, so worthy. Roger whispered more soft words in her ear, and she took to them like a cake to icing.

"Roger, I do love you," she said with all her heart.

"I love you, Selina. Tell me, my darling, that nothing will ever make any difference."

"Nothing will ever make any difference," she complied. Then she asked: "But what could?"

"Money. You see" ... a little pull to his mouth ... "I haven't any."

"I don't care."

"But" ... painfully ... "*you* have—at least will have money."

"I still don't care," she insisted.

"But don't you understand, Sellie, *I* do. *I* care."

"Then, darling, you mustn't. It could make no difference. It won't happen, but even if it did happen, *it would make no difference*."

"You know, I think you mean that, Selina."

"Mean it? I mean every breath of it, Roger."

"Then I think we can take it that we're engaged." He tilted her chin to look into her eyes.

"Engaged? Oh, Roger!" For Roger had drawn from his pocket a little velvet box and in the box was a ring.

"Don't—don't you have to ask Unk or something?" All at once Selina found herself hesitating. She could not have said why.

"You're of age, and anyway, he's not your guardian. Also, to be quite frank, Sellie, I wouldn't be absolutely sure that Claud Whittier would be on my side."

"On your side?" What was this—a battle?

29

"If he would approve of me," Roger explained.

"Of course he would. He couldn't help it." Yet still that finger of hesitation touching her.

"So, my sweet," Roger went on, "it might be a good idea not to wear this openly yet, a good idea to let him get used to the fact of us more gradually."

"Yes, Roger." There was relief in Selina, and there shouldn't be relief, she thought uneasily, there should be a protest, a denial, a proclamation that she intended to do no such thing as wait, that she was going to shout it from the treetops right now. Shout it from the very top of the ledge.

Which, and Selina considered it distastefully, was Redgum Ridge. Now why had she thought of that?

"I think, Roger, you'd better keep the ring here until we—well—"

"I think that, too, darling. See, Selina, we are one already."

"Oh, Roger, I do love you," she said again.

"And you know how I feel."

"Red hair and all?"

He did not answer that, instead he said: "I have some special shampoo, Sellie, I'm sure it will work, take out any unwanted colour."

Shampoo. Soft hands. Manicure. Why were these foolish things running through her mind? It was the man who mattered, and Roger was the man. Unk might have his doubts, but she *knew*. She accepted Roger's bottle of shampoo, listened to his instructions on how to use it, returned his goodbye kiss, then left.

The expensive Grant car was still on the drive when she got back, but as she approached the house the owner came out and got in.

"I'm taking your uncle down to Tallow Wood tomorrow," he told Selina.

"I could have done that," she retorted.

"As a matter of fact, you couldn't, you're barred."

"Barred?" she queried.

"I'm not, I'm what they call a disinterested person, a bystander."

"What on earth are you talking about?"

"Come for a ride with me and I won't tell you."

"You're mad!" Selina said crossly.

"Well, I can't tell, it's not my affair, but come anyway, Red."

"Red?" she queried.

"Or Ginger?" He was looking impertinently at her. "It's hard, actually, to tell."

"Yet you should be able to, being Red Indian."

"Your own peculiar way, I think, of saying that I'm a savage."

"Primitive," she agreed coolly, "barbarian, uncouth."

"That's enough." He smiled implacably. "I have the general trend. But give me time and I'll improve. You see, while your Roger has been at finishing school—"

"Forestry Academy."

"I've been cutting sleepers."

"But many years before," she corrected pertly. "Roger isn't thirty yet."

"How old am I?" He asked it idly, yet his eyes were narrowed on her almost as though her answer mattered.

"As old as Redgum Ridge," she shrugged back.

"That's as old as creation itself. We're so old in

Australia we're up to the process of being worn down to the beginning again."

"Well?" she asked coldly.

"Well, I can tell you, Selina" . . . Selina, indeed! . . . "I'm not being worn down, not yet. Savage, primitive, barbarian, I may be—"

"You forgot uncouth."

"Also" . . . ignoring her . . . "a one-time cutter of sleepers, but even though I'm no real Red Indian, there's still red blood."

"Cut yourself and show me," she begged impertinently.

He secured the door of the car, evidently convinced she would not accept his invitation.

"Any cutting I do," he told her, "will be to you." He paused. "Down to size, young woman."

He released the brake and was accelerating along his private road before she could think of an indignant reply.

CHAPTER THREE

SELINA supervised the children's lessons from nine till noon. It was done on one of Tall Tops' large verandahs to afford the pupils a feeling of school by having to leave their homes. Selina knew from her own learning days that arranging one's books on the kitchen table in one's own house wasn't quite the same as a classroom, even an improvised classroom on a verandah. However, her mother had been a good supervisor, and she hoped she was the same.

All the children had smaller brothers or sisters, which made it an excellent arrangement all round, since a supervising mother with a baby to watch as well cannot hope to concentrate on her child as an unburdened, unmarried young woman can.

Selina loved the chore she had taken upon herself. As Iron Grant had remarked, she liked children. He had remarked more than that, she remembered with a flush, he had said: "We two should think over that mutual liking one day—do something about it." The nerve of that man!

None of the pupils were at the same standard, but it did not matter that the impetus of competition was missing, since correspondence depended entirely on individual effort.

The smallest children were not up to correspondence, but Selina had accepted them to take them off their mothers' hands. They were very easy, anyway, all they required was a sand tray and some building blocks. She often said ruefully to Uncle that at least she was equal to their intelligence.

"Don't sell yourself cheaply," Uncle had returned. "As far as I could tell from the little I saw of your sister Madeleine, you would run rings round her, flash boarding school and all."

"I don't know," Selina had doubted. The few times in the earlier years when Maddie had come home had marked Madeleine clearly as someone who certainly knew her way about . . . and who also knew what two and two make, Selina half-smiled now.

She had not heard from her sister for years. Madeleine had married at eighteen after she had enrolled in a university in the States, another whim that Uncle had financed rather than have a discontented girl back at Tall Tops. Selina had only learned about the marriage after she had cabled Madeleine about their mother. Maddie had since moved on, and it had taken a while for the news to catch up. By then Madeleine had finished that marriage, then married someone else. Maddie's comment on this in her answering letter had been 'More fool me'. It seemed to indicate that this marriage, too, was foundering.

"Poor Mummy," Maddie had finally written, "too young to die, even though her years sound dismaying at our stage of life. Will you stay on, Selina? Though I expect you will. Besides your being a bird and mountain lover, it should be to your advantage. The old fellow, I remember, had no one at all of his own. Well, all I can say is you jolly well deserve it."

"Miss Lockwood," called Janet, "how do I spell spectacular?"

"You have your dictionary, Janet."

"But how can I look it up if I can't spell it?"

"You'll still find it. Michael, stop putting blue crayon on Phyllida's hair."

"But she likes it. She said so. Blue is the latest hair colour. Why don't you use blue, Miss Lockwood?"

"Because I don't use any—" Selina stopped. The beautiful eyesight of children would have caught her red gleams at once, for she still had not got round to using Roger's special shampoo. She would try it as soon as lessons were over. Uncle had left very early with Iron Grant for Tallow Wood, and Tallow Wood was a longish journey, which would leave her plenty of time to work on her hair with the added advantage of no one round to comment.

"Play-lunch," she called, and went out to the garden for a breath of mountain air ... and the sight, perhaps, of Roger.

At twelve o'clock the children wandered home, but it took Selina the best part of an hour to pack away the little ones' blocks and sand tray, and to fold and encase in their official envelopes the older children's lessons to be sent to Sydney for correction. After that she made straight to the bathroom, put out a supply of towels, filled the basin with hot water, then uncorked Roger's shampoo. She poured more than she should need, for she wanted to make a really good job of it this time, and was soon wearing a thick halo of bubbles. The perfumed soap dribbled into her ears and cut out all sound, so that she heard no steps coming down the hall. As for seeing, does anyone see through shampoo?

But *feel*, Selina did. She felt fingers taking over her

35

job for her, and after her first surprise she thoroughly enjoyed the service. Going to a hairdresser's was something that only happened when she went down to Tallow Wood, and, very appreciative now, not one of the girls had ever given her a scalp-tingling clean-up like this. Roots finished to Roger's satisfaction, every strand of hair was brought individually forward, rubbed, scrubbed, tweaked, rinsed, then the process repeated all over again. Finally came the towelling, and Roger . . . trust Roger . . . had placed the towels over the hot rails so that the impact of the absorbent cotton was comforting as well as drying.

Then what a towelling! Up and down, side to side, round and round. Finally head right over so that the under tendrils that usually dripped uncomfortably long after the rest of the head was finished would be as dry as the top.

Dear Roger. Dear thorough Roger. Dear . . . The sting of soap had left Selina's eyes now and instead those eyes were wide open. She was looking at the hand assiduously rubbing her. Square-cut nails. Blunt workmanlike hands, rather ruddy brown in colour. An axeman's hands. Definitely . . . *definitely* no fastidious care here. No manicure. She struggled free of the towel and looked up.

"You," she said blankly.

"Who did you think?" asked Iron Grant. "Oh, of course. I should have guessed when you stood so docile."

"I wouldn't have had I known."

"But why not? I've given you your money's worth. If I'd been an attendant in a saloon, Miss Lockwood, and have charged you for the time I have taken on you, you wouldn't have enough left over to add a tip."

"I would never add a tip—to you."

"And yet I've made an excellent job of it. See for yourself." He pushed her to the bathroom mirror and forced her to look at her drenched reflection.

"See, not a whisper of red," he indicated, "not a hint of ginger. Tell me, did any of your pupils notice this morning?"

"No, of course not . . . I mean, Michael did suggest blue."

"Then they noticed." He nodded. "But not tomorrow, for again you'll be peeled twigs."

"That's Uncle's description," she said tightly. She felt a fool talking to the mirror but a bigger fool still thinking it had been Roger all the time. If she had only known she would not have stood quiet like she had.

"Yes, Claud has a nice turn of phrase," Iron was saying. "But not just now. The old boy's tuckered out from Tallow Wood, and told me to tell you he's going to snatch a kip. And that, if you require an explanation, is why I'm now in your bathroom. I came to deliver the message, Miss Lockwood."

"What's wrong with Unk?" she asked anxiously.

"Nothing. Good lord, the man is well over eighty, and it's a twisty road to Tallow Wood. He's entitled to a rest."

"Yes," she agreed, "but I still think Unk—"

"If it's lunch, then don't think. We ate down there. He doesn't want any more, he wants a rest. If you come with me for that drive I offered you and you refused yesterday, you'd make it a better rest. You're not exactly silent around the house, are you? I tracked

37

you here at once."

"Because the tap was on."

"I've heard you at other times. You sing."

"Because I'm happy," said Selina deliberately and
... she hoped ... significantly, and had the pleasure of
scoring from a definitely unpleased look on his face.

"What's wrong?" she asked too innocently. "Can't
I be happy?"

He answered carelessly, quite without intention ...
yet there was no mistaking an intention there.

"Only with me," he said.

"Mr. Grant—"

"Joel. Iron if you must."

"Mr. Grant, you're being quite impossible!"

"Just because I ask you to come in the car to ensure
a quiet house while your uncle sleeps?"

"You know that's not what I meant."

"But it's what I'm meaning now. That other can
wait. Will you?"

What other could wait? She looked at him irritably.
"No," she said of the drive. "My hair is wet."

"After any towelling of mine, no hair is wet."

"I want to set it," she insisted.

"The mountain wind will set it. The sun will shine
it. If we return at dusk you can fasten in the evening
star for a clip." Now she looked at him incredulously,
and he nodded back. "Oh, yes, it's me. You don't
have to be a graduate to string fancy words, even
sleeper cutters can do it."

"Very clever of you, but I still won't be coming."

"A pity. Your overseer is."

"Roger?"

"Yes. I'm taking him up on my railway to show

38

him where I intend to tip his sawdust spoil. He will have to see to the loading of it, of course, he can't have it all his way all the time. But in spite of that disenchantment he's quite keen. Your young friend has a modern outlook, Miss Lockwood. He approves of mechanism. He has no time for bullock teams."

"With a train you would be modern, too," Selina snapped. She always had regretted Roger's dislike of the old jinker.

"But still with a lot of time left for such nostalgic things. You see" . . . a pause . . . "I grew up on them."

"One of a large struggling family," Selina suggested pertly, "living in a little bush shack. Very poor."

"Why don't you provide music to it?" he asked sharply, and she could see he was angry with her.

A little ashamed, for after all it was not in good taste, she said : "I would like to come, please."

"Because of the overseer?"

"I'd like to go on the railway."

Abruptly he tossed : "All right, then. The car's in front."

They took the private road, but they did not go as far as Iron Grant's house. They turned off before then and drove to a clearing, where another car already waited. As they pulled up, Roger got out of the car and greeted them.

This, Selina saw, was the basal point of Iron Grant's mountain railway, the point to which Tall Tops, further down the valley, would have to build their line. The actual junction must already have been agreed upon between the two men, for Roger took out a graph he had done, and Grant perused it and nodded. Meanwhile Selina looked around her; she had been once to the Redgum Ridge house but never on the property.

There were blackbutts as well as the redgums that had evidently given the place its name, and they were so tall they seemed to vanish into the sky like Jack's beanstalk. There seemed to be no shortage of trees, yet Iron Grant dealt commercially with many more than did Tall Tops, any of the surrounding lumber camps. Evidently Grant believed, like Uncle did, in planting a new tree every time a tree was felled.

She heard a grunt and a puff and saw Billy . . . mountain trains just had to be Billy . . . descending to a small platform a few yards away.

"First class or second, madam?" asked Iron Grant, and bowed Selina aboard.

She sat in the front with the driver, who was Jock, Joel Grant introduced, and the iron man and Roger sat at the back and talked about loads and gradients and running costs.

From where they boarded Billy it was a hundred and thirty feet to the top, and every inch was vertical. Billy, as was only to be expected with such a gigantic effort, panted and puffed out every fraction of every inch. It was a little scarey travelling vertically, Selina found, but so beautiful you soon forgot. She had thought it was wonderful down in her tree world, but up here it was pure enchantment. You became a close neighbour of the peaks around you; where the peaks cut at the sky you could almost reach out and feel the serrated edges. You were in a blue world.

When Billy reached the top there was another platform, but Iron Grant shook his head and indicated shining lines that had been newly set.

"We'll continue on, Jock," he called, "and show Tall Tops why we'll take their sawdust."

About a quarter of a mile on, the line stopped . . . and the beauty as well. There had been a landslide at some time, and though the rawness had worn off there was still a gaping and unlovely hole.

"I aim to fill it up," said Iron Grant, "then leave it to nature and the trees to do the rest."

Roger said knowledgeably: "But you won't get anything choice here, Grant."

"By choice you mean—?"

"The finer stuff. The softwoods—cedar, maple."

"You don't call the hardwoods choice?"

"No."

"Then you're wrong. I'm on to something very choice. Look." He nodded further down the scarred hill.

"Blue gum." Roger was patently unimpressed.

"A whole valley of blue gum, and with a higher-yield eucalyptus than I've ever found yet. It must be the location, it must suit these blues. Why, the oil isn't just waiting to be won, it fairly oozes out. It's all very crude so far, but the potential's there. Are you aware of the price of eucalyptus now?"

"Yes," admitted Roger.

"Come and I'll show you," Iron said.

Selina and Roger followed Joel Grant down the raw hill. At the bottom there was a crudely built hut that made Roger visibly wince. But he could not refrain from being impressed with the fifty-gallon drum of oil that Grant showed him next.

"Just ten days' work," the iron man grinned.

"But what work!" Roger was teetering between

dismay and envy.

"But what a price!" Iron grinned again.

"You'd need a good return," Roger said a little pettishly.

"You sound as though you know the process." The older man was lighting his pipe.

"Days to cut the leaf, days to cut the wood, days at keeping the fire burning," recited Roger. "Then piping off the vapours, condensing them."

"Finally collecting the fat cheque," and Iron smiled all the way this time.

Selina was looking at the red tips of the blue gums' leaves, she was breathing in gum tang, which, she had decided long ago, was the very breath of heaven. She had noted that all-the-way smile and been disgusted. Money, money, money. Everything this man did was for money. She picked a sprig of gum and snapped a leaf to sniff it.

He must have been watching her, have read her disapproval of him, for he addressed himself now to Selina.

"You just wasted several cents of oil, Miss Lockwood."

"I'll pay you, of course," she flashed.

"Of course, or I'll have it out of your hide."

She looked at him incredulously, then looked around for Roger to back her up, but Roger was exploring further down the scarred hill. She went and joined him, hearing softly, for her ears alone, Joel Grant's low bantering laugh.

When Selina reached Tall Tops again, Uncle Claud was sitting on the verandah, and he looked particularly well. He was in an expansive mood and asked

Roger to stop for a drink . . . Iron Grant had not come back to Tall Tops . . . and when Roger accepted, he was very pleasant with his overseer.

"Uncle, you *can* be nice when you like," Selina beamed after Roger had left.

"Of course I'm nice. I've had a nice life. Your nice mother saw to that when she came along one day and brought with her a nice girl."

"Two nice girls." Selina felt she should say that.

"Don't know about that one," Unk shrugged, "I only know I was as glad for her to go to that flash boarding school and later that American university as she was. If she ever complains, young Selina, just point out that she cost me about as much as I'm leaving you."

"Oh, Uncle, not that again!"

"Don't want to lose me, eh? All right, we'll talk about other things."

And talk he did. He talked of their valley and how it had looked when no man yet had stepped into it, of the first bush humpy to be built, of the first axe-ring in the clear sweet air. Of the bullock teams, not just one team like they kept now for the hard-to-get trees, but teams of teams, because there was no mechanism then. Of the ringing oaths of the bullock drivers.

"Also," went on Unk, "no mechanical saws."

He talked into the night, the night that Iron Grant had suggested could provide Selina a clip for her hair. He told dingo stories, snake stories, a story about a convict who had lived in a hollow tree-trunk for five years. Then he talked about his trees, of the men who had cut them. Some of them had been chip-mad, he said, not good clean deep cutters. Generally the chip

43

ones, he went on, had chips on their own shoulders.

He said a few things that Selina could not follow ... like it being the best way, and she would know it was so in the end. Then he leaned back and talked about the Big Feller, the grey gum whose ancestors had been pushed out of the white gum community, the boyo, who, just to spite the whites, had reached up two hundred feet.

"Too big for his boots, Selina," he said, "but Joel will never lop him."

"Joel? Mr. Grant?" She looked inquiringly across ... then she got up quickly.

"Unk. ... Uncle Claud!"

But she knew even as she said it that he could not answer her. It was as quick and as final as that. The old tree had fallen just as Unk had wanted to. No axe. No saw. No mill. Only the wind.

"I'll plant orchids," Selina said foolishly as she ran to the phone and began to dial.

A voice answered and she said a few incoherent words. But she must have been understood, for the voice said: "I'll come at once."

She ran back to the old man, and only then did she realise that she had dialled Redgum Ridge and not the overseer's cottage as she had intended, she had called to Joel Grant, not Roger, for help.

Instinctively she had looked up, not down. Up to Grant's, Ironbark Grant's, the sleeper cutter.

Why? *Why?* Selina asked herself.

CHAPTER FOUR

BUT it was Roger to whom Selina turned in the days that followed. Angered at the somehow *essential* way she had appealed to the big man on the ridge almost as if something intrinsic had compelled her to, Selina now determinedly consulted Roger on the smallest issue, had him by her side for the most trivial detail. Roger in return was anxious to help. Every problem was promptly taken away from Selina, a solution found to her approval. Roger was gentle, solicitous, patient, loving, and Selina told herself that she loved him more than ever. She loved his sympathy, his aid, his comforting presence . . . but it annoyed her that Joel Grant was frequently present as well.

She knew she had only herself to blame for this, it had been her own foolishness in calling on him on the night of Uncle's death that had started it. She would never understand *why* she had reacted like that, *why* she had done such a thing as telephone him before anyone else, but she did know that the happening had had its repercussions. The man simply came to Tall Tops and went from Tall Tops as he pleased, almost, she often fumed, as though he believed he was entitled to, as though it was his place. Roger did the same, of course, but Roger was different. She might not be the future mistress here, even though everyone seemed to expect and accept that she would be, but she was the mistress *now*, and, as such, her fiancé was where he

45

should be, by her side. But it was different for Iron Grant. If events turned out as it seemed they would, then Roger must tell Mr. Grant he was not wanted. Though surely, Selina often thought, that man would understand that in marriage (if not in pre-marriage) a third is distinctly unwelcome.

Roger wanted the ceremony as soon as possible, but though Selina was of the same mind, she still hesitated. She felt for form's sake they should wait a while, and was relieved when Roger, always conscious of convention, quietly agreed. How awful, she thought, if Roger had been a man like—well, like Iron Grant, someone who sneered at niceties, who rode roughshod over things, who insisted that this was today, not yesterday.

She was particularly pleased that Roger conceded without any trouble, since otherwise she might have had to hint to him Uncle Claud's dismay when she had spoken to Unk of herself and Roger. Why, she wondered . . . she was posing herself a lot of questions lately . . . had Uncle gone on as he had that day? He could not dislike Roger, no one could, and Roger had proved himself a skilled worker, really a perfectionist. Perhaps, though, Uncle had later turned the page on that little outburst, for he had not mentioned the subject after that and he had been quite congenial with Roger. Congenial with everybody, especially on his last night, bless him. He had been completely unworried then, almost as though his trip down to Tallow Wood had taken a load off his mind, though, and Selina grimaced, a trip with that man would only give her a load.

Though Roger spent his time with Selina, he did not neglect his own work. He apportioned the supervising jobs that he always did himself to his immediate subordinates, and concentrated instead on Tall Tops.

One morning Selina came out and saw him estimating the big grey gum.

"He's far too large, Sellie."

"Yes, Unk always said that, he always said 'too big for his boots'."

"Well, we must do something about it, mustn't we?"

"What do you mean, Roger?"

"We must cu—" Roger must have seen a look in Selina's face, for he changed it at once to a diplomatic: "We must lop him."

"Oh, no, Roger!"

"Then shape him, trim him a little. Be reasonable, Sellie, one branch is over the eaves and you'll have a cluttered guttering."

"No!"

"Darling, I only said that not to alarm you, but now I will alarm you. For your safety, Sellie, he must be lopped. That branch is quite perilous."

"But, Roger, he's only a young tree, he doesn't need pruning, he's as firm on his feet as I am."

"*Are* you, sweet? Come clean now. Aren't you a little giddy with love, Selina? I know I am."

"Oh, Roger!" She appreciated the way he conceded to her at once. I'll make it up to him some day, she thought. Such kindness can't be one-sided. She slipped her arm around him.

In their absorption neither of them heard Iron Grant coming round the side of the house.

"I thought I was at the back garden of a place called Tall Tops," he called, "but I must have lost my direction, instead I'm at Lovers' Lane."

They had separated by now, and distastefully Selina said: "We were just discussing the big grey gum. Roger considers it should be lopped."

Quite coolly Iron Grant drawled: "It won't be, though."

Although he spoke without heat there was no mistaking the intention in his voice. Roger looked at Selina, and Selina, after looking back a long incredulous moment at Roger, glared at Iron.

"Well, *I* think it might be a good idea," she said defiantly.

The man pulled out his eternal pipe and took his time over it before he answered.

"Then think out some other good idea," he advised.

"You—you must be meaning the permission councils or shires demand these days for the removal of trees, sometimes even the lopping of them. But good heavens, a forest holding doesn't come under a council or shire ruling."

"Keep talking," Iron invited.

"I'll do nothing of the sort, and I think you should do the same. After all, it's no business of yours."

"It is." Still he appeared unperturbed, for that matter only faintly interested.

"Oh, I know you were a crony of Uncle's," flashed Selina, "but don't let the friendship of an old and ... let's face it ... no longer *discerning* elderly gentleman give you ideas that you can air your own ideas."

"Oh, I won't." He glanced up from the pipe. "But" ... the pipe lit at last to his satisfaction ... "the tree will still not be touched. Now will you step inside, Miss Lockwood. I have a few details to discuss."

Selina knew he meant the memorial service that had still to be conducted in the small bush church·on the way to Tallow Wood. Though Uncle had been laid to rest in its acre, it was still an established thing that afterwards the mountain men gathered together on their own accord. Transport was difficult up here for the majority of the woodsmen, it was not just a matter of taking a car, a train, a plane, or even in several instances a helicopter, since a lot of the old foresters who had served Uncle lived in remote valleys, valleys from which they could only climb out of by jinker, or haulage truck. Yet they would all want to say goodbye to their old mate.

Finding time to grimace secretly at Roger, Selina followed Iron into the house. She squirmed, as she squirmed frequently of late, at the rather proprietorial way that Iron Grant went into the study. He nodded to a chair, and she sat down sulkily. He sat down himself.

Uncle's small funeral had taken place nearly a week ago now. Lighting his pipe, Iron proceeded to tell Selina that the service would be exactly a week after.

"By that time all who can come will have done so. I've had letters from as far as South Australia—"

"*You* have?"

"I," he reminded her levelly, "inserted the notices in the different interstate papers, so it was only to be expected that I received the replies." As she did not comment, he went on: "Also there were several from Victoria and Tasmania."

"You should have included New Zealand papers, Uncle worked in the forests there, too."

"I cabled there," came the calm reply, "and several

old mates are flying over."

"In short you've covered everything."

"Not everything. Not yet." A pause. "Your sister, Miss Lockwood."

"Madeleine? But I hardly think Madeleine—"

"But you don't *know*, do you?"

"I believe I do. She hated the bush as a child, so I scarcely imagine—"

"Children grow up. She might have different ideas now. But different ideas or the same ideas, I think she should be here."

"Why?"

"You need another woman."

"There are plenty of women. It's only in the bachelor chalets that there are not any women."

"Allow me to finish, please. You need another woman *in the house*. For one thing, a lot of the visitors will have to be billeted here."

"Then Madeleine will be useless, she always fled from domesticity," Selina pointed out.

"There are other reasons for another woman in a house as well as home duties. The role of chaperone, perhaps?"

"Chaperone?" she gasped.

"Presumably all the visitors will be male, so it would be scarcely the thing for you to be the only other member of the opposite sex."

"Are you serious?" Selina asked in disbelief.

"Yes."

"Then indeed you did have that remote childhood." She smiled quite impertinently. "I can see it all, Mr. Grant. Father no doubt at the head of the table in that humble bush hut, Mother at the foot, children with their rules of behaviour in between."

"Are you trying to be funny?" he asked.

"Not trying, because I think it's all riotously funny. The backwoodsman emerges from yesterday ... *but not quite*." Again the impertinent smile. But the smile faded as he leaned over and took hold of her wrist. The grasp was hard as the tag he went by: Iron. It was iron-hard.

"Yes," he said very quietly, "you could call me an old-fashioned man."

A silence fell, but like all the silences up here, it was a loud quiet. The leaves in the trees talked to each other, crickets whirred, birds twittered, a down valley stream chimed out waterbells, children raised their voices.

"Your sister is coming." Iron Grant broke the silence.

"You really mean you would like her to come. Well, I'm sorry, but I can't supply Maddie's address. She hasn't been in touch for years."

"I have the address. I've written. She arrives today."

"*What?*" she gasped.

"You heard me, Miss Lockwood. By devious methods, I won't waste time telling you now, I found out that she had returned from overseas. I contacted her and she was pleased to agree."

"Oh, yes," said Selina bitterly, "she would say that to a man."

She became aware that he was looking at her quizzically. "I used to think that the female sex was the gentle sex," he drawled. "No, I had no experience of women as a child, my mother had died, and there were never any sisters, brothers, either, for that matter,

51

but now I see differently. You're as brutal as the male."

"Brutal?"

"Where is your sisterly love? You should be looking forward to the reunion."

"Perhaps I would if it hadn't been taken out of my hands. Anyway, the reason for Madeleine is ridiculous. I need no chaperone, particularly when——"

"When?"

"When I'm shortly marrying Roger." There, it was out. Selina sat back and looked challengingly at him.

He did not answer at once. When he spoke at last it was slowly, carefully. He said : "I wouldn't bank on that."

"What?"

"Your friend the overseer, to say the least, is—changeable."

"Changeable?" she asked.

"Take the grey gum, for instance, he soon changed his mind about that."

"But he didn't. You said very autocratically : 'It won't be touched', then gave him no opportunity to answer back."

"He changed his tune," Iron stuck out. "By not speaking himself he established that fact. And once a changer, always a changer. Be warned, Miss Lockwood."

"You—you're abominable!" she said angrily.

"I didn't go to the Academy," he returned blandly, "so what can you expect?" He waited a moment, then went on, "Your sister arrives in the Sydney plane at three this afternoon. I'll go down to Tallow Wood and bring her up. Will you come?"

"No. I'll have to prepare her room."

"Get some of the women to help you prepare several rooms then, there are sure to be a few pilgrims on the plane come to say goodbye."

"I wish—" began Selina, then stopped herself. She had actually started to say: "I wish I could bid you goodbye." What right had this preposterous man to take over everything?

She got up abruptly and went out of the house. She looked for Roger. When she found him in the shrubbery he was mending an old bench that had seen better days. She could hear him tut-tutting quietly at the bad repair, and she smiled fondly. Everything about Roger, even his tut-tuts, was quiet, controlled, gentlemanly. So different from the sleeper-cutter. Roger straightened at that moment, and the fair hair that had fallen over his brow righted itself again. How good-looking he was. How very nice to have about you, to show to your friends. But to show to your sister? Selina stopped in her tracks.

Madeleine, she was remembering hollowly, Madeleine at seventeen, which was the last time she had seen her. Shining copper hair, not 'peeled twigs', dancing cornflower blue eyes, not steady grey. As beautiful a girl as any girl could hope to be and any man could wish a girl to be.

Selina looked at Roger and felt a finger touching her heart. How would Roger who liked everything to be beautiful, to be the best, regard Madeleine?

Roger, at this state, was quite gratifyingly annoyed at the idea of Madeleine. Selina, who instantly put Roger's dismay down to a reluctance to have anyone else around with his Selina, glowed with happiness,

and did not hear anything amiss in Roger's perturbed:
"What does your sister think she'll get?"

"She's beautiful, Roger," Selina said, tucking her
arm in his.

"I won't see it."

"You'll have to see it. She's a bird of paradise,
Roger, compared to a brown wren." Selina was wondering wistfully if some of the copper of Maddie's
glorious hair had faded, the eyes as well. But, she
faced up, you could always fix hair, fix eyes, too, for
that matter, with skill and with shadow, and Madeleine
would certainly have the art. Oh, Madeleine, don't
get ideas about Roger.

Roger was saying encouragingly: "My dearest, you
have all I could ask for—I dislike flamboyance. But
I must add that I think it was bad taste of Grant to
ask your sister here, and certainly not his prerogative.
—Selina, is there any possibility—any likelihood of—"

"Yes, Roger?"

"Your late uncle, dear. The will."

"Oh, no, nothing would be left to Madeleine."

"Madeleine? I once knew a Madeleine . . ." For a
moment Roger did not seem to be with Selina. Then
he recovered himself, returned to the present and kissed
her.

Coming out of the house at that moment Joel Grant
called: "Lovers' Lane seems to have changed its location. You two should put up a signboard to warn
trespassers away. I'm leaving for Tallow Wood to
collect your sister now, Miss Lockwood. Prepare at
least four bedrooms. If more old mates arrive on the
flight, I'll ring from town." He wheeled round and was
gone before they could say a word back to him. But

54

they said a word to each other ... many words.

"Really, Selina, that man should be put in his place!" Roger said angrily.

"I'm expecting you to do that, Roger, as soon as—well—"

"He goes on as though he owns this property. I've never seen anyone presume on a friendship quite like he does, even if your uncle was alive it would be abominable, but to persist after someone has passed on is really beyond the pale. You're right, it will have to stop, and I'll have pleasure in stopping it. Sellie, how long now? I understand your sense of fitness, darling, but you can see for yourself that apart from us loving each other, that man is making a fool of us."

"Soon. Very soon.—You see, Roger, I hesitated before because—well, because Uncle had reservations about you." She had not wanted to bring it up, but now it seemed she had to.

"What do you mean, Selina?"

"He seemed to think you wanted what came with me, or presumably came with me, as well as me."

"That was damnably unkind," said Roger, and he looked sensitively away. Presently he turned and gulped: "I must admit I would like to make a success of it all for you, Selina, but surely I can't be blamed for that."

"Blamed! Darling, I *praise* you for it. Take no notice of poor old Unk. He was sweet, but he was elderly, and—well, you understand."

"The only thing that matters is what you yourself understand. Understand about me. Tell me it's a good worthy understanding, Selina."

55

"It is, oh, it is, Roger. I'll marry you any time you say. I feel different about it now. I know that Uncle would have been different had he had longer, poor dear, and less time under the influence of that man." Selina looked at her watch, then sighed.

"How long," she asked, "to get five bedrooms ready?"

"Five?"

"One, of course, for Madeleine."

"Driving a car of the kind he drives" . . . an envious note in Roger's voice . . . "less than three hours. I mean, there won't be any shopping at Tallow Wood, will there? Just direct to the field, then back. In which case I wouldn't count on a leisurely preparation, Sellie. Look, dear, I'll help you."

Giggling, Selina refused. "Our sleeper cutter wouldn't approve of that. He's an old-fashioned man."

"So am I, Selina," warned Roger with delightful mastery, "but, like our backwoodsman, I like things done properly. Ties tied properly. Selina, we'll be married today week if that suits you."

"Oh, it does!"

"Your sister can be your bridesmaid."

That did not suit so much, but Selina encouraged herself by remembering that copper hair can fade, corn-flower eyes grow less radiantly blue.

. . . Most of all that in a week's time it would not matter, for she would not be Miss Selina Lockwood any longer, she would be Mrs. Roger Peters.

CHAPTER FIVE

THE billets were finished just as the big Bentley swung into Tall Tops drive. Four men ... Selina was glad she had prepared five rooms ... alighted.

And Madeleine.

Iron Grant did not get out of the car. He sat behind the wheel and watched sharply, shamelessly, and with unconcealed enjoyment. Watched Selina's reaction to her sister. For if Madeleine had been lovely before, now she was something of which dreams are made.

Her hair was more copper than ever, her eyes if not bluer, as Selina knew they could not be, then certainly bluer with their subtle turquoise shadow, with their fabulous fringing lashes. For the rest, Madeleine was as slender as ever, as graceful as ever, but infinitely better presented. She had always had a flair for clothes, but now as well as the best boutiques of Sydney to assist her, she had the know-how of London, Paris, New York. The old woodsmen, come to pay their respects to Uncle, were obviously dazzled.

Selina, wishing that Iron Grant would stop looking like a Cheshire cat and instead move off, kissed Madeleine, told her hastily she would get the old men settled first, then busied herself performing the settling.

They were all old dears. They could have come out of the same mould as Uncle Claud ... wiry, hard, spare, calloused, slow of speech as people are slower away from the hurly-burly, thoughtful from years of estimating a tree's height and the way it should fall. They all patted Selina's hand and asked would it offend her if they kipped for a while, for they were not, they reminded her, young saplings any more, and needed their rest.

"You poor old trees," Selina smiled. She knew the language. She took in a cup of tea to each of them, then closed each door. Then she turned to Madeleine.

"At last!" her sister grinned.

"Well, Maddie, they've come a long way."

"I know. I got it all on the plane. Thank heaven they're bedded now and we can talk." Madeleine lit a cigarette and regarded her younger sister. "You've turned out better than I thought," she observed.

"Was I that awful?"

"You were terribly childish for your age. You're a bit immature now, but the promise is there." Madeleine grinned again.

"*You* are a riot." Selina found she had to say that.

"Not bad, but it does keep me busier than it used to maintaining the standard. You get a bit sick of it at times. When I got Joel's letter" . . . Joel already! . . . "it was like manna from heaven. I'm not usually a mountain and tree lover, but I was a bit sick of city concrete."

"Have you been back in Sydney long?"

"Under a month. I returned after Rod and I split up."

"Rod?" Selina queried.

"Number three, dear, and good riddance to him. I think I'm going to enjoy a rest here for a while, particularly with a Bentley owner like Joel about."

"Mr. Grant comes from Redgum Ridge."

"Oh, yes, I know all that. He told me everything on the way up." Everything? "Quite a dish if you go for the masterful type, which I do. But what about you, darling?"

Selina said: "I'm engaged."

"To that masterful type?"

If Grant had told her everything he would have told her that, thought Selina. She answered: "Oh, no. To Roger. "Look" . . . drawing Selina's attention to Roger walking through the garden down to his villa . . . "there he is."

There was silence from Madeleine. It became such a long silence that Selina turned and looked at her sister. But the girl was only ashing her cigarette.

"Name of?" she asked casually.

"Roger Peters. He was Uncle's overseer. Academy type."

"Yes, I know that. I really mean" . . . a little hurriedly . . . "you would know, wouldn't you, just looking at him."

"Yes, just looking at him," Selina agreed proudly. No railway sleeper stuff there, she thought.

Madeleine turned a little abruptly from the window and said: "So you had the right idea after all."

"What, Maddie?"

"Staying on. Digging in your toes. Oh, I'm sorry, pet, you do genuinely like it, I can see that, but you must admit it has paid dividends."

"If you mean Tall Tops—"

"I do."

"Then I don't know anything yet."

"You mean the will hasn't been read?"

"No."

"But you're pretty confident of the result?"

"I wouldn't say confident, Madeleine, but everyone seems to think—"

"And you, what do you think?"

"Frankly, I don't know, and I don't really care, so long as I don't leave my timberland."

Madeleine looked at her with amused pity. "You do really love it, don't you?"

"Yes."

"But for all your unworldliness, Selina, you still must have a clue."

"About Tall Tops?"

"What else?"

"Well, Uncle did say once" ... an apologetic pause from Selina ... "that you, Maddie, shouldn't complain, because he had spent as much on your upbringing."

"Could be," admitted Madeleine, not at all put out, "that school was so exclusive even I was out of face at times, and it takes a lot to rattle me. But" ... a shrug ... "little good it did me. The same for the university. Three men and not one sou settled on me from any of them for the simple reason that they hadn't any. Your big sister proved herself a bad chooser. Better luck next time."

"Next time?"

"Darling, I'm still only twenty-six." Madeleine looked at Selina with estimation. "You must be twenty-two."

"Yes."

"You look like a kid taking a break from her gym tunic for the day."

"I look older with make-up," Selina argued.

"I should hope so, you'll get nowhere as an ingénue."

"Oh, but I have. I have Roger."

". . . Yes." Again a pause. Presently Madeleine said : "While you're doing the million and one things that have to be done with guests in the house I'll go down and meet this Roger."

"I'll come and introduce you."

"Darling, since when have I needed introductions?" With a little low laugh Madeleine departed, leaving a faintly uneasy Selina standing at the window. She saw Madeleine go across the garden, then up to the door of the overseer's villa, saw the door open, saw Madeleine disappear inside.

More than faintly uneasy now, Selina turned back to perform the 'million and one things'. The therapy of work! Selina was so busy for the next hour she completely forgot her unease. She saw to the evening meal, buffet and cold to help everyone relax, then one by one greeted the old woodsmen as they came out of their rooms to sit on the verandah and smoke and yarn. Particularly yarn.

What stories they had to tell! Mostly about difficult cuts, long haulages, snakes, dingoes, the advantage of hickory over gum and of American axe handles over Australian or ones from New Zealand, for there was one Kiwi among them. Many of the tales Uncle had told Selina before, but many were new, frequently blatantly untrue but very good listening. One by one she identified the old fellows. . . . 'Woody' Glenner who still flew up from Gippsland every year for the Sydney Royal Show axe events but these times only as an adjudicator, 'Timber' Benson whose record for the Undercut had never been bettered, 'Chip' Summers from New Zealand kauri country, though undoubtedly *he* had never had a chip on his shoulder, 'Savage' O'Reilly, the meekest-looking man Selina had ever seen.

"Yes," the others agreed when Selina said this, "but you should have seen him with a saw. Three big blocks to be severed. He was quicksilver, and look at the lumbering luke he is now."

This was the time for beer, definitely beer, not any of Roger's fine wines, and Selina brought the bottles out and left the old woodsmen reminiscing. She felt cheerful again, almost as though Unk was by her side and saying proudly to them : "This is my sapling." She was cheered again by the sight of Madeleine and Roger coming across to the house, a full yard apart, and patently uninterested in each other. Perhaps Roger had been speaking truly when he said he disliked flamboyance.

But if Roger disliked it, someone else quite openly appreciated it. Iron Grant did. He drove down later, and he did not try to conceal his admiration of Madeleine. Madeleine responded enthusiastically, and the two paired off. That left Roger for Selina, which was what she wanted, so why— Why?

The following day the minister arrived from Tallow Wood and the service for an old woodsman was conducted in the tiny bush church off the Tallow Wood road. The Reverend Bill Flett had been born in timber country, and, apart from college days, had served in timber country all his life. He could have been a woodsman himself with his bark-brown eyes and his estimating look, but instead of estimating a tree's height, he estimated people. He began with Deuteronomy. ". . . for the tree of the field is man's life." He used phrases the foresters knew and liked, he said of Uncle Claud : "Not sawn, not axed, just fallen in the wind."

Then he finished with Revelations. "Hurt not the trees."

Noses were blown, though Savage O'Reilly openly wept, then they were all out in the sunlight again, because, unlike the deep valleys, there were few trees here to make it a green instead of a blue and gold world, and Iron was waiting with his Bentley to drive the old boys back to the Tallow Wood strip.

They all kissed Selina, looked dazzled again at Madeleine, and then the big car was turning the bend and beginning the big descent.

Madeleine, Roger and Selina walked back to Tall Tops. Roger put Selina in the middle and every now and then he caught at her hand. I needn't have worried, Selina glowed.

The rest of the week proceeded quite pleasantly. Although she was no help in the house, Maddie was amiable enough. The old Maddie who had grumbled about everything from spiders to mill dust seemed to have gone. The girl was obviously appreciating the quiet after years of jet living.

Then the following morning among the letters, mostly condolence, that Sam brought up from the Tall Tops box on the Tallow Wood road, there was an official-looking letter for Selina. The way you do, even though you know it seldom reveals much, Selina turned the letter over. But this time it did reveal something, it told her it came from Nossiter and Nossiter of Tallow Wood. Neil Nossiter had been Unk's legal man.

Selina opened up the letter.

"Miss Selina Lockwood, Dear Madam" . . . though he had known her for years, indeed since she had come here, Neil was always very correct professionally . . . "You are hereby requested to attend the reading of the will of the late Claud Whittier at two o'clock on Wednesday 15th, at this office." Then: "Yours etc."

Attached, Neil had written: "If you can't make it, ring me, Sellie, and we'll fix another date."

"Can you make it?" Madeleine, to whom Selina had read the letter, asked idly. Madeleine knew she was not concerned, so she was not particularly interested.

"Yes," Selina said.

It was three more days till Wednesday, and Madeleine and Selina spent the time looking at the long-forgotten corners (forgotten by Madeleine) of Tall Tops.

"Though I doubt if I ever looked into any corners," confessed Madeleine. "All I wanted was to get back to the city again."

Her sister was behaving quite beautifully, Selina had to admit. Madeleine visited the married chalets as well as the bachelor ones . . . the bachelors were no chore . . . patted the heads of the children, took a ride in the jinker and helped down in the nursery. She spent more time in the nursery than Selina expected of her, but that would be because Iron Grant had come down on his side of the fence. The two talked for a while, then the man whistled across to Selina.

"You can whistle!" Selina fumed. "Whistle, my lad, and I'll come doesn't refer to me." She added mutinously to herself: "Oh, no, my lad!"

However, Madeleine came across and told her that Joel wished to speak to her, so Selina put down the seedling tree she was about to insert in the rich waiting soil, and strolled across.

"You had a letter from Nossiter?" he began.

"Did Madeleine tell you?"

"No, Neil did himself. He rang me and said you would be down for the reading on Wednesday."

"Neil did that!" she gasped.

"Why not?"

"Well—well, it sounds unethical, to say the least."

"When I am the executor?"

"The—?"

"Executor. Kind of trustee. Sort of general watchdog to see things are done right."

"You!" she exclaimed.

Again the man said: "Why not?" When Selina did not answer, he pointed out that someone unrelated was generally preferred.

"I'm unrelated," he concluded.

"So am I," Selina said.

"But you are concerned with the actual will, I am not."

"You seem to know all about it, though," she commented.

"I know nothing, nothing, I mean, that's concrete."

"But—implied?" Selina slipped in.

"Look, I don't wish to discuss that, I'm just telling you that as executor, trustee, guardian—"

"Sort of general watchdog," added Selina icily.

"Exactly. I just want you to know that I'm expected to be there."

"Then you'll have to be, won't you, but what beats me is why . . . that is if I'm really concerned—"

"You are."

"Why I should need a—dog. I'm not a child. In fact I am well and truly of age. *Over* age. I'm twenty-two."

"I know your age," he said, "but I also know that Nossiter has asked me to be present. Foolish to take two cars when one is sufficient. Shall I call for you?"

"I suppose so."

"Then Wednesday." He turned away, drew Madeleine's attention to some young tree he was planting and did not address Selina any more.

It was all very irritating, but as Roger said when Selina told him later, it had to be.

"I was wondering," Roger added, "when the law would make a move."

He himself moved constantly around Tall Tops, pointing out to Selina things that should be done. He was right, of course, Uncle had not believed in change, but, as Roger said, you simply had to progress with the times.

To Selina's surprise, Madeleine did not express any wish to drive down to Tallow Wood with them. Tallow Wood was no hub of activity, but at least it did have a small string of shops, and Selina had expected that Madeleine would have been anxious to see them. On her arrival she had only seen the Tallow Wood strip, which was some miles from the town.

But Madeleine was not at all interested. "Corny stuff," she demeaned. "In the end I would only be

66

sitting waiting in your solicitor's office, waiting for you, and solicitors usually have such dreary magazines. No, I'll lie back here and relax while you collect your shekels."

"Oh, Maddie, not shekels!"

"Well, valleys of shekel-producing timber, then. If you see something exciting you can buy it for me as a consolation prize."

"Oh, I will, Madeleine, but Maddie, I don't want you to think——"

"That I'm deprived? Darling, I was joking. I've had my share. Anyway, we don't know yet, do we, *what* Uncle had to leave. Maybe the place was mortgaged or something, maybe you're only getting a leaf or two to press and keep in your Bible."

"So long as it's a leaf from The Big Feller."

"What do you mean?"

"The grey gum," Selina explained.

"The one Roger says will come out?"

"Roger," said Selina, annoyed, "changed his mind about that." But she was mostly annoyed at the fact that Roger had been discussing the tree with Madeleine.

Madeleine said quickly: "Come to think of it, it was I who said it. A twig fell on me. It could have been a branch."

"With a koala clinging to it."

"Stop joking, it might have been serious."

"But it's not being removed . . . well, not according to the big boss of Redgum Ridge." Selina was remembering that incident with Iron Grant.

"And where does Joel come in?"

"Probably he's a tree trustee or something."

"As well as your trustee. Darling, don't explode. You look as though you will at any moment. Also, don't worry about me on Wednesday. I'll find things to do."

But the thing that did worry Selina on Wednesday was the sight of Madeleine waving to her and Iron *from Roger's verandah.*

She soon forgot it. No one, and Selina had learned it years ago, could descend to Tallow Wood and remember anything but beauty.

Trees followed them almost into the town, nature's, not man's, trees, mostly eucalypt, their grey-green leaves because of the oil in them now released by the wind and the sun giving out a soft blue look. But there were palms and limes and the silver surge of many streams racing down gorges as well, deep valleys full of lacy shadows, mountains with necklets of trees on their soft breasts. There were, as they came nearer to Tallow Wood, grassy carpets of foothills, then the smooth flats that comprised the small but important timber centre.

Neil Nossiter greeted them: "Hi, Selina, howdy, Joel," but once inside his office he was very correct. He read aloud in a dry legal voice, pausing every now and then to make sure that Selina was following.

It was easy enough to follow. She was the sole legatee. All that Uncle Claud had possessed was left to her.

"Trees," she smiled.

"Well—" Had Selina been sharper she would have seen an exchange of looks between the two men.

But—"Trees are all I would want," Selina prattled on. "I was always aware that the mountain was

68

Crown-owned."

"No," Neil Nossiter came in at once. "That law was relaxed some years ago, and Claud Whittier immediately applied for ownership and was accepted at an agreed sum."

"You mean—"

"I mean it became entirely his, not leasehold any more. He paid an estimated figure for it, estimated by the Government, but what it was worth privately later was a very different amount." He looked guiltily at Selina to see if she had caught that 'was' instead of 'is', that 'privately' and that 'later'. When he saw she hadn't, that she was still abstracted, he said : "Miss Lockwood, Tall Tops today is worth over one hundred thousand dollars."

"One hundred—" But Selina found she could not get beyond that.

"Riches, isn't it?" Neil permitted himself to smile. "Especially since that sum represents the selling price after all the usual legal costs have been taken out."

Selina's confused : "I beg your pardon," and Iron Grant's quiet : "Later, Neil," came exactly at the same time.

Neil only responded to Iron's injunction. He agreed : "Yes, perhaps you're right." He waited for a few moments. "But immediately," he went on presently, "before you start doing any handsprings—I really mean before you start making any plans, there's a provision."

"A provision?" asked Selina.

Neil Nossiter looked down to his desk, cleared his throat, then read the rest.

"... to Selina Lockwood, I give, devise and be-

queath the whole of my estate both real and personal"
... Neil glanced up again ... "upon her attaining the
age of twenty-five years—"

"Twenty-five?"

"Yes, Selina."

"But—"

Neil held up his hand, then before she could speak
again he finished: "... upon her attaining the age of
twenty-five years before she marries."

"Before I marry! But—"

"In simpler terms," said Neil, "you must remain a
spinster for" ... he looked inquiringly at Selina ...
"how many years?"

"Three."

"Three. Now that's a mere bagatelle."

"But I'm engaged to be married, Neil."

"Of course. No objection to engagements. But
marriage only in three years' time, otherwise ..."

Selina corrected bleakly: "Three weeks, not three
years. No—three *days*!"

"Well, not now, Selina, because if that happens
the money goes automatically to a specified cause. I
have it here." Neil Nossiter looked it up and announced: "Tree husbandry."

The solicitor's substitution of 'money' for 'estate'
or 'property' or even 'Tall Tops' passed Selina by as
had the other things he had said. Selina had other
matters on her mind.

Three of them. Years. Three years before she and
Roger could marry, unless—

Unless she forfeited.

CHAPTER SIX

"WE shall still be married," Selina said stubbornly on the way back to the mountain.

"Such a proclamation is certainly your privilege," acknowledged Iron Grant, "yours—and his. I take it you do mean Peters?"

"Of course. Roger."

"Then your privilege—and Roger's."

She caught the quiet implication in his voice and turned angrily on him. "You think Roger won't want to marry me now, don't you?"

"Yes," baldly.

"He loves me."

"If you say so."

"I do!"

"Then he loves you." A shrug. "But he's still a very practical young man, and a hundred thousand dollars can buy a lot of desirable things."

"The only thing we both desire, as well as each other, is the timberland, and the only reason we would delay anything . . . though we won't . . . would be Tall Tops. Tall Tops alone might make us think twice."

"Then I suppose I'd better clear up something there," said Joel Grant, and he ran the tip of his tongue round his lips in a preparatory manner.

But he never said what he had to say. The occupants of a car on the side of the mountain track attracted their attention, and the next hour was spent trying to coax a sulky engine to spark again. When finally it did, and they resumed their own way, they were both absorbed in their own thoughts and spoke only sparsely.

When they got to Tree Tops Roger was away directing the laying of the little set of lines to join up with the Redgum Ridge lines, so Selina had to wait to tell him. She could scarcely go down to the clearing and blurt it out, even though she was tempted to. She longed to say what Neil Nossiter had told her, then feel Roger's quick arms around her as he assured her : "We won't wait that long, darling. We can't. Damn the inheritance !"

What would they do instead? Well, smiled Selina confidently, that was easy. A graduate like Roger could get an overseer's position anywhere, and though it might have to be away from here, it would not be away from her beloved trees, for trees, thank heaven, were Roger's livelihood.

Then even if fate cruelly decided that Roger should fill a city job instead such as a lecturer, or somebody on the executive staff, then, though it would be a wrench, she loved him enough for city life as well.

The tension of waiting for Roger to come up from the line laying proved too much for Selina. She found herself babbling it all to Madeleine.

"A hundred thou !" Madeleine gave a long unlady-like whistle.

"But only if I wait until I'm tweny-five to be married."

"That's nothing," Madeleine dismissed with the experience of three marriages behind her.

72

"It is when you love someone. You must have felt like that once yourself."

"I doubt if I could have held out against a hundred thou, unless it had been for—" Madeleine gave Selina a quick look, then shrugged.

"Don't be a fool," she resumed presently. "The time will fly."

"I don't want my life to fly, I want it to come slow and rounded and perfect and—"

"Sellie, shut up and listen to the voice of wisdom. It's just not worth the sacrifice. I'm sure Roger won't want marriage, anyway, but still don't tempt him."

"You're speaking just like Iron Grant did. Why shouldn't Roger be agreeable?"

"Because he wants to be successful. I mean" . . . hastily . . . "successful for you as well as for himself, and Tall Tops isn't exactly something that falls into your lap every—it was three years you said, didn't you?"

"Yes. Three years. When I'm twenty-five and still unmarried. But you're so wrong, Maddie. Roger will be disappointed, terribly disappointed, he loves this place like I do, he's already worked very hard on it, *but he doesn't love it that much.*"

"We'll see," Madeleine said. After a while she asked: "What did the Iron Man have to say?"

It was only then that Selina recalled that Joel Grant had begun a: "Then I suppose I'd better clear up something there," then been diverted by the car. It had come after her declaration that only the ownership of Tall Tops might change the minds of two lovers. What had Iron Grant been about to announce? she wondered.

It seemed hours before Roger returned to his over-seer's villa, and yet it was only the usual time. Selina did not wait for him to shower, dress in the attractive casual clothes he always did, she went across at once.

"Roger! Roger!"

"Darling!" in protest. "I'm all sweaty. Give me ten minutes at least."

"No, Roger, we must talk now."

"Really, Selina, is it that serious?"

"Yes . . . yes, it is," she insisted.

Roger looked grave now, and he crossed at once to Selina's side.

"The will was not what you expected?"

"I hadn't expected anything, you know that."

"Of course I do, dear, but you understand what I mean."

"Yes, I understand, and no, Roger, it was not what I expected."

"He—Mr. Whittier never left his estate to you after all? Or did he share it with Madeleine as well?" An odd little note in Roger's voice, had Selina only heard it.

"Oh, no, I was . . . am . . . the sole legatee. But—"

"But?"

"But," she blurted, "I have to wait, Roger."

"Wait?" he queried.

"Wait till I'm twenty-five."

"Three years, Selina? Oh, well, I guess we can do that."

"I haven't told you everything. I should have said I have to wait until I'm twenty-five to marry, otherwise—"

"I see," said Roger. He then said: "Yes, of course."

"Of course?"

"That was your uncle's way of compelling you to think twice about me, make sure."

"Oh, darling, as though I would need any time! As though I'm not sure. I love you as you love me, without any side offer of a hundred thousand dollars."

"*What*?" he exclaimed.

"That's the amount Neil Nossiter mentioned."

"They must have had the property valued," frowned Roger.

"Yes," said Selina vaguely. "Oh, Roger dear, it is a disappointment, isn't it, but we'll find something. I thought today as we drove down to Tallow Wood that though we think we have the best spot here, that though we feel there is nothing else quite like it, there still is, and there must be. There must be somewhere as good. There are lots of corners, Roger, and if we're together the corner we finally got would come to mean much more to us than this place. Because it has our love. Because it's us."

She became aware that Roger was not listening to her. He was running his fingers through his thick fair hair that he always kept very neat and controlled.

"Roger!"

"Sorry, Selina, I was miles away."

"In our little timber valley of our own?"

"Well—no."

"Then overseer to some other big timber holding?"

"No."

"Then" . . . a little disappointed but brave . . . "a city executive job?"

"No. No, little Sellie, I was just thinking of us waiting patiently, which is what, of course, we will do."

"Roger—" she began.

"Oh, I love you, Selina, you know that, but good heavens, girl, I couldn't pass up...I mean you couldn't pass up...one hundred thousand dollars."

"I could. I am."

"No, Selina, you are not. Selina, look at me, my sweet. I have brains, I have ability, but what else have I to offer you?"

"You yourself, Roger."

"Always an employee, never an employer?"

"Then love, Roger, you have love to offer."

"But it has to be more than that, Selina."

"It's enough for most people," she argued.

"But most people aren't heiresses. Selina, I have talent, but I'm still, in these days of automation, potentially redundant. Where would you be if all at once we were married and I was out of a job?"

"I could work."

"You could be out of a job as well."

"Then we would still exist, Roger, exist together. Roger, I can't understand you, it's been you all along wanting to hurry things up, and now...and now..." Selina's voice broke and she began, very softly, very heartbrokenly, to cry.

Roger knelt down beside her. "Little Sellie, don't take it like that."

"What other way is there to take it? Money, money, money, it's not important."

Roger looked at her shrewdly, only through her tears Selina could not see the cool estimation.

"No, money isn't...but Tall Tops is. Selina, I—I love this place. I—I—" He turned away, and by the defeated hunch of his shoulders, Selina could see he

76

was deeply distressed.

"Oh, Roger," she forgave him at once, "it was not what I thought, it was—it's—"

"Yes, darling. It's the mountain where I first met you. But as you said just now all places can be precious, so why be stubborn about this one?"

"Yet we still know in our secret hearts that it *is* different, don't we?" Selina said quietly. "We know our mountain is the only mountain. You're right, Roger, it will be dreary to wait, but it will be worth waiting for. Oh, darling, forgive me."

"Forgive you? How can you ask that of a man covered with mill dust and ashes?" He laughed and kissed her. "Give me those ten minutes, sweet, and we'll go up to the house." He paused. "Our house?"

"In three years' time, Roger. Will I be old and grey by then?"

"Not if you take after your sister Madeleine."

It was a slightly discordant note, but Selina decided not to hear it.

"Ten minutes from now, then," she stipulated. "If you're not ready then I'll come and drag you out of the bath."

"A promise, not a threat," he agreed, and the next minute the shower was running. He emerged immaculate and co-ordinated as ever, olive-green scheme today, slacks, shirt, cravat.

From the verandah of Tall Tops, Madeleine . . . and Joel Grant who had come down from Redgum . . . watched them approach.

"Going by their wise and calculating looks tree husbandry will *not* be receiving a large bequest," Joel said laconically.

"No," agreed Madeleine, and no one could have said whether she was pleased or not.

The four of them had drinks on the verandah and talked about everything. Everything, that is, except an inheritance a girl had received today. Three of them drank a little too much and became a little reckless in their speech. Madeleine made atrocious jokes. Roger said some extravagant things. Selina babbled. But Iron Grant remained very cool, very restrained.

Finally it was Roger who mentioned legatees.

"Will our little millionairess . . . no, it's only a hundred thousand, isn't it? . . . then will our little hundred thousandess still supervise school?" he laughed.

"Why not?" Selina laughed too gaily.

It was then that Joel Grant came in.

"It depends on where you are, doesn't it?" he said. They all looked at him, even though he had addressed himself only to Selina.

"I'm not sure if all lumber camps run to a supervisor," he went on, "or whether Tall Tops is unique in that respect. However, if you thought of remaining in the district, perhaps renting one of the huts, even taking a room at the overseer's villa, if he's still there, you could still carry on, Miss Lockwood. Personally I quite like the idea of a lesson supervisor, I'm all for education, having had little myself, and not being an Academy man." He kept on talking in that strain, knowing they were not listening, knowing they had absorbed only that one sentence:

"It depends on where you are, doesn't it?"

A minute went by. There was no joking from Madeleine now, no extravagant talk from Roger, and Selina was silent. No one took up their glass.

"Cat got your tongues?" Joel, who had finished what he had to say, could have directed that to anyone, for he looked straight ahead. Presently he went on : "To relieve this unbearable tension I'll say something that I intended to say this afternoon, only I was sidetracked. It is, of course, to do with this property."

"Tall Tops?" It was Selina . . . faintly.

"Yes." A pause. "It's mine, you know."

If he had made the announcement any other way, made a statement of it, a declaration, it could not have been more dramatic. But the casual, almost offhand information came like a sudden trickle of ice-cold water down your back on a hot day.

"Yours?" It was Roger.

"Yes."

"That's why Nossiter could give Selina the exact amount?"

"Yes, that was the sum I paid Claud Whittier, plus the usual legal fees to the solicitor on top of it, of course. Claud wanted a round figure for Miss Lockwood."

"It's a lot of money to pay." It was Madeleine.

"But a very fair price. I'm not a fool, I would never let sentiment blind me however much I desired a place."

"Sentiment?" At last Selina found her voice.

"No. Delete that, please," Iron Grant said harshly. "Get back to the amount. As I said, it was fair, and I was satisfied. After all, Tall Tops covers a deuce of a lot of space. Good space. Good trees."

"Trees," echoed Selina, and her voice cracked.

"Quite right, Miss Lockwood, every tree for as far

79

as you can see belongs to me. Every leaf on every tree. But not to worry, you have, or will have, your hundred thousand dollars."

"You—you put Uncle Claud up to this!" she accused.

"I did nothing of the sort. I always wanted more land, and I simply made him an offer and he accepted."

"But why? *Why?* He knew I loved the place."

"But he did, too, he loved it, I mean, so naturally he had to safeguard it."

"Safeguard it?"

"From anyone else who might not love it as much."

"As much as you love it?"

"Yes, as much as I love it."

"But Roger loves it."

"I'm sure," was all Joel Grant said blandly. After a while he drawled: "Surely you must have caught on when I made myself so much at home in the place. Do you think I would have done that if it hadn't belonged to me?"

"I don't know what you would do," Selina said. "I—I don't know what I'll do." She got up abruptly and ran into the garden. It was elf light but fast growing dark. She found the grey gum, but it was a case of groping for it with tears blinding her eyes. She threw her arms around it.

Roger found her there. To her surprise he was not disconsolate, not—not wrecked as she was. That could mean only one thing, it must mean that without the prospect of Tall Tops there was nothing to keep them waiting any more.

"We'll let him have it," she cried almost in relief.

"It appears we have to," he reminded her.

"I really mean we'll leave the mountain and start together as I said we would before you talked me out of it. We'll be married, Roger."

"No," he told her slowly and very distinctly, "we will not . . . not for three years. Then after that time we'll get married, darling, for then, my own Selina, we'll be able to buy Tall Tops back from him for ourselves."

"What do you mean?" she asked.

"I've watched Grant closely. I always have. He's like many unfinished men, and by unfinished I mean self-taught, non-degree men, he has the natural material in him, but, Selina, you need much more than that."

"He's made a success of Redgum Ridge."

"He's been lucky there. He hasn't used modern know-how, only his experience, and though he's got through, it's only been because he had a good run. No, my dear, you can take it from me that knowledge must win in the end. Listen to me, Selina, three years is not too long, not long *to have each other and the place we love.*"

"But how could we have it?"

"Simple, darling. Ironbark Grant might be able to run one holding, but never two. He would be incapable. I know his type. He'll be glad to sell."

"But to us?"

"Not many people can hand over a hundred thousand dollars."

"But, Roger—"

"Then we—I mean you, dear—will own Tall Tops. We will have each other and our dream as well."

There was something wrong somewhere. Surely if Roger loved her, *really* loved her, he would be thinking of nothing else.

Perhaps she would have said so, but at that moment the leaves in the big grey gum stirred in the evening breeze, and one of the branches seemed to reach up to entangle the young sliver of new moon.

No, Roger was right. She could not leave this place. It was worth scheming for, waiting for, so long as in the end she ... and Roger ... were here. Here together. And yet, and she said so unhappily to Roger, it appeared that she would still have to leave Tall Tops. For three years, anyway, until she could claim her money, then buy out Iron Grant.

"No, darling, after you left us something came up. Grant himself suggested it. He wants me to stay on. Obviously he doesn't like me, but he does seem to have a sneaking respect for my work."

"But what happens to me? Do I disappear? Do I take a world trip or something? But I couldn't do that until I got my money, so what do I live on for three years?"

"You stay here, too."

"No!"

"But you love it."

"And hate him."

"I put that wrongly, sweetheart, I should have said 'But you stop here and love me'."

"Yes, Roger," Selina gulped.

"Then there's something for you, too. Give it a hearing, anyway, and Sellie, if you can, answer Yes. Please, Sellie, for us."

82

"For us," she agreed, "that is if it's not too—too—"

"Come up and hear it," he pleaded. He led her back to the house.

Madeleine and Iron Grant still sat on the verandah, although it was quite dark by now, the dark of tall places, where, when the moon came up, you felt you were already halfway there to pluck it down. Also, the trees gave out so much oxygen you became a little heady with it. The tang of leaves, sap and moss caught sensuously at you. The velvet of the shadows touched you.

Oh, Selina thought, I can't leave it.

Iron Grant began at once. He used no preamble.

"I've told you that Tall Tops is mine, so we needn't go over that again, over the why and the wherefore, I mean." He took out his pipe. "What I want to talk about is my plan for the place. It's this: I want it to go on as it is right now."

"You mean—you won't be living in it?" It was Selina.

"Haven't I a place of my own?"

"Yes—but—but otherwise why did you buy it?"

"Because there are some fine valleys and some wonderful heights, some promising afforestation."

"I was meaning—the house?"

"Now that," said Joel Grant, tapping the pipe, "is something altogether different."

Selina waited . . . the three of them waited, but the sleeper cutter simply worked on his pipe and offered no more.

Distastefully Roger said when at last it appeared

that Grant would not broach it: "And Tall Tops'
overseer, Mr. Grant?"

"You'll stay. Claud Whittier had nothing against
your work. A few personal ideas of his own as to how
he would have done it, perhaps, but nothing serious."

"Thank you." Roger's voice was thin.

"Miss Lockwood, too, will stay on. I like the idea of
the school—I said so before. Also, I want the house
kept as it is now."

"Very well." Selina's voice, too, was thin.

Madeleine broke a little silence.

"That only leaves little me," she complained plaintively. "I know I'm only a visitor, not official, but—"

Joel Grant turned quite amiably on her. For a
stern man, thought Selina, it was astonishing how kind
and tolerant he was to Madeleine.

"Waiting for me to give you your marching orders,
eh? Well, my dear" . . . my dear! . . . "I'm not. From
the look of you" . . . his eyes travelled up and down
the lovely woman . . . "you would have a lot of know-
how in a house."

"If you mean," broke in Madeline, alarmed, "cooking and all that—"

"No, I don't. I mean dressing a house up."

"Interior decorating?" Madeleine glowed.

"Yes. I have up there a big shell with nothing in
it. That's an exaggeration, of course, it's furnished,
but it could do with a finishing touch. Many finishing
touches."

"Oh, I'd love that, Joel."

"You can come up during the day, then."

"Come up?" she queried.

"Well, you're not stopping there," grinned Iron

84

Grant very meaningly, "not until I make up my mind, madam."

"As to what?" Madeleine grinned back.

"We'll see." The big man rose. "I'm going home now. It's been a big day. A big day, too, I would say, for our heiress." He looked deliberately at Selina.

Selina said: "Not that yet."

"No."

He nodded to each in turn, then went down to his car.

They sat on in silence, until Roger, too, rose. Despite the fact that his clothes were impeccable as ever, somehow he seemed crumpled. Madeleine, getting up as well, had lost her gay mood.

"We haven't had supper," Selina said . . . but said it to herself. Roger had crossed to his overseer's villa and Maddie had gone to her room.

Selina stared out into the darkness, dark, that is, except for necessary lights, for power was used carefully up here since they were dependent on their own plant. If only, she thought hollowly, I could forget inheritances, forget money. Forget tomorrow. Why, oh, why can't I stay at now?

No, not now. Now is almost as bad as tomorrow, because it is full of the waiting for tomorrow. I wish, Selina thought finally, I was back at yesterday.

CHAPTER SEVEN

BUT you could not live in yesterday when you were surrounded by children. Children never remain static, all the time they are growing, expanding, becoming seven instead of six, or nine instead of eight, becoming different small identities, since children alter with the years.

Selina reluctantly admitted this and accepted today ... but she still would not think of tomorrow. Tomorrow was three years away when officially she could marry Roger as well as collect her inheritance. It all sounded very neat and tidy, just like Roger ... but was it something of the heart? That was what fretted Selina. I'd like, she thought, unreasonably and unpractically, for someone just to say to me: "Marry me *now*."

But Roger didn't say it.

Joel Grant did, though. He must have been in earshot when she grumbled her thoughts aloud, he was often at her—at *his*—house these days, and he said at once:

"*I* will marry you now."

"Do you always overhear?" she demanded crossly.

"When it's said in an overhearing voice."

"I never meant it to be."

"Well, I meant my response. The inheritance, or lack of it as it would be in such an instance, wouldn't dismay me."

"Naturally, when you're in a different category, when you have more than enough already."

"So," he ignored, "damn tomorrow and marry me now."

She knew he was baiting her, but nonetheless she carried on with the ridiculous topic.

"I wouldn't marry you if—"

"Spare me the rest. I've heard it all before. It runs ... 'if you were the last man on earth'."

"Oh, so you've had your share of rejections."

"Frankly, no. You, if you reject me—"

"Of course I'll reject you!"

"Will be the first. But I have read time-honoured replies by heroines in books."

"Those kind of books would be novels."

"Then novels."

"You read novels!" she jeered. "I only expected treatises on trees."

"I know all that gen already."

"Self-taught!"

"Exactly, Miss Lockwood." He gave a challenging grin. Presently he asked: "Why the bellyache?"

"What do you mean?"

"The whinge. The whine."

It was no use trying to deceive this man, so Selina did not try.

"I'd decided not to think of today nor of tomorrow but to live in yesterday."

"And you find you can't?"

"You try it with children!"

"I'm glad you brought up the subject of children. You're to have another one." As she raised her brows, he proceeded: "We have a new man at Tall Tops."

"You mean you have."

"I'm corrected." He bowed. "The fellow is a Ukrainian, name of Anton Wolhar."

"Yes?"

"He's a good forester. Not just a good worker but a good woodsman. You don't turn anyone down like that."

"Why should you turn him down?"

"Because he brings a child with him."

"His?"

"Not exactly. He married only recently in Sydney. A Polish widow with an eight-year-old boy, Ignace."

"Yes?"

"There was a tragedy. A car ran off the road on to a pedestrian walk and killed the new wife at once. Anton and the child, who were walking with her, were untouched. Now Anton is here at Tall Tops to work. He has brought Ignace."

"I see no difficulty in that, in fact I think it's a wise move on Mr. Wolhar's part. He'll be doing work he understands and will not have to cook his meals and the boy's meals as he would have to in a city, for I think you would categorise him as a bachelor, Mr. Grant, and so eligible for bachelor services." By this Selina meant the big mess where an extremely good German cook saw that the unmarried foresters of Tall Tops were well nourished.

"No, no trouble there, but trouble for you."

"How do you mean?"

"Young Ignace speaks no English. He also, as is to be expected, speaks no Ukrainian. Any communication between Ignace and his stepfather has only been brought about by close association and much gesticulation. But you, Miss Lockwood, will have to start off from scratch."

"Poor little boy," said Selina softly. She added: "Poor man, too."

"Yes, it was Anton's first marriage, and I think he was deeply in love. But he can speak English, if disjointedly, so can talk with those around him, release some of his feelings. The child is all alone."

"He won't be for long. Children never are."

"This means you don't object?"

"Of course I don't object. Ignace must come along tomorrow."

Ignace didn't come, but Selina did not worry. She knew that the little boy, shut up in an un-understanding world, must take his own time.

She told the other children about Ignace, but they were not very interested, they were more interested in his stepfather.

"Mr. Wolhar," said Shelley with awe, "is carving a tree."

"It's a blackbutt," went on Michael, knowledgeable, as the child of a woodsman should be, when it was trees.

"You must come down and see it, Selina."

They all went down to see the tree, and since Anton Wolhar had worked an early shift, he was there himself, with Ignace. Ignace immediately hid in some bushes, but Anton good-humouredly ignored his stepson and told Selina about the tree. He was chipping a totem into the solid trunk because he liked doing things like that and because it entertained Ignace. Later when Ignace did not need entertaining, at least he could look at the tree and say with pride: "My stepfather did that," because what Anton had chipped and carved was an old Polish ancestor.

"My dear wife told me about Svantovit, who was worshipped one thousand years ago in her country. The name means 'He Who Can See the Whole World' and there must be four faces on the tree looking on four quarters. Later Svantovit should hold a bull's horn, and my dear wife said that after wine was poured into it, if it remained until the following year, the year would be fruitful." Anton touched his carving with pride.

"Mr. Grant very kindly has approved of me doing this," he said, "not just to help me forget some of my sadness, but to help the boy. For this totem is early Polish, and this boy is Polish." He smiled at Selina. "Ignace must be proud of that as I was proud of my dear wife."

"It's fine," applauded Selina sincerely, and, seeing Ignace's small nose pushing out of a bush, she said: "Ignace must come up to the verandah tomorrow. I can't give him lessons, but he can be with the other children, play with the little ones' sand box and blocks, look at the books."

"I will tell him that—oh, yes, we can tell each other things. But speak properly? Not yet."

Ignace came shyly the next day, and fitted in quite well at first. But he was eight, not four, and after a few hours on the sand tray and at the blocks, he became bored with such baby pastimes. He waited until small Lucille had finished a castle, then he scrabbled it down, he let Bobby build a tower, then removed the bottom block.

"Please don't, Ignace," called Selina.

Ignace, who must have understood Selina's tone if not her words, did another awful thing. He took the big, very beloved teddy bear . . . every pre-school class must have a teddy bear . . . and hung him on a tree *upside down*.

"You're a bad boy," reprimanded Selina.

Ignace smiled angelically back at Selina.

Still, it could have been worse, Selina thought, seeing both hands of the clock at twelve. She dismissed the class.

But alas for Selina's 'worse'. Though Ignace appeared to have been absorbed by the smaller children's sand tray, blocks and bear, he was a very intelligent eight-year-old and the frustration of seeing other girls and boys working with pencils and paper where he was excluded filled him with a futile rage. What he needed was a migrant class first, but how could he know that, and who, up here at Tall Tops, could tell him? could teach him?

He had been watching Selina enclosing the class's papers in the Government envelopes to be sent down to the State Correspondence School for correction. Suddenly he ran across and grabbed them from Selina, then bolted.

Selina bolted after him. This was a serious matter. The Correspondence School expected the papers to come in at a certain date, they would ask questions when they did not. If the children did them again, they would feel it an unfair chore, tell their parents, and their parents would object. Selina's only hope was to get the papers before Ignace tore or burned them up.

But the little boy did neither. He put them down

the toilet . . . and that made it worse still. It was, as was to be expected up here, a septic system, something that had to be treated with respect and care and most certainly not stuffed with paper. Seeing Selina close on his heels, Ignace shoved in all he could, then pulled the chain, and that at least helped save the day, since the septic simply could not take such a load.

Selina withdrew the papers at once, wondering desperately whether she could dry them out . . . wondering what she could do about Ignace, because one simply could not ignore anything like this, wondering—

But Ignace helped her there. He must have sensed the seriousness of his act, for he brought along his stepfather. Selina explained at once, and Mr. Wolhar proved very helpful in spreading the papers, fanning them, at last taking them into the big laundry . . . blessedly empty at this shift . . . and ironing each sheet dry.

It was all over half an hour after it had begun, all except the punishment of Ignace. Selina looked at the Ukrainian and the Ukrainian looked back at Selina. He knew, as Selina knew, that a lesson must be taught.

"Come, boy," he said.

Then something awful happened, or that was what Selina thought at first. Anton took Ignace down the valley and cut a big stick, then very soon afterwards Selina heard some loud whacks. They were extremely severe whacks, far too severe for a child . . . for anyone. Selina cried: "Oh, no—!" and ran out of the laundry and into Iron Grant's arms.

"What in tarnation—" He must have heard the whacks, too, the cries.

"Anton Wolhar is thrashing Ignace...oh, it's awful!"

"What did the kid do?"

"Nothing. I mean, he put the class papers down the toilet, but nothing...I mean, we fixed it up all right." Selina's last words were to nobody. Joel was racing down to where the sound of the punishment seemed to be centred. Selina rushed after him.

They were so quick about it, Anton Wolhar had no time to stage a deception. He was already staging one, but he had no time to stage one to conceal the first deception. He had the big stick all right, but he was whacking a dead trunk, and Ignace was watching on, and every now and then yelling in pretended pain.

"What is all this?" Joel called.

Anton threw away the stick and looked stricken. "He has been bad, very bad, but how can I thrash him? How can I, Mr. Grant? He has no mother. He cannot tell me even how he misses her. I cannot understand if he does."

"Even if you did understand him and he understood you, I hardly think a stick of that size—" said Iron.

"Then?"

"A slap, of course. A good spanking."

"You will give it?"

"Not now, Anton, it has to be done at once, not half an hour after. Anyway, I think I have a much better idea. It certainly worked on me."

"What, Mr. Grant?"

"Ignace likes pudding?"

"Too much. He hurries his meat and vegetables for ice cream and pie."

"Today," said Joel, "no ice cream and pie."

At that moment the whistle went, the middle of the day whistle meaning 'Tucker's on, come and get it'. Ignace ran eagerly up to get it, and he did get meat and vegetables. But no pie. It did not need Anton's gesticulations to tell him why, or Selina's frowns or Joel Grant's severe looks. Ignace, intelligent as Selina had guessed, caught on at once and hung his head.

"He won't do that any more," said Iron, as he and Selina went up to the house.

"Where did you get such knowledge of children?" she asked. She had been quite impressed.

"The same way as I got my timber knowledge, through myself."

"You were deprived of pie?"

"Yes, for a punishment, and I soon caught on."

"But I thought there were no women in your life."

"A kindly neighbour used to send over apple pie. I adored it."

"And learned your lesson when you didn't get it?"

"Yes." A small nostalgic smile, the first time Selina had ever seen this big tough man look backwards. "I often think of those pies . . ."

Selina could not have said why she did what she did do that afternoon. It came so naturally and so instinctively that she never questioned it. No, she did not make an apple pie. They had no apples. But they did have blackberries down the mountain.

She went into the blackberry valley with a billy can and a stick, for snakes like to sleep under blackberry bushes, and there in a sun-splashed corridor of trees she picked fat berries, heavy with syrup, from the wild bushes. It was quiet in the grove. The only sound was the pleased exchange of birds feeding busily, the occasional plop of a too-plump berry to the ground. Suddenly Selina felt happier than she had felt for weeks. She looked down on her hands, her fingers stained with purple, and had the feeling that she held all fulfilment in the blackberried hollow of her palm.

She climbed back to the house and made a blackberry pie, and because she had been well taught by her mother it was a lovely pie. Flaky, light, oozing with dark fruit and luscious juice.

Iron Grant had remained on at Tall Tops to see to some item needing his attention, but towards evening he returned to his car. This was the time she usually stood at the window watching Roger come up from the valley. Today instead she took out the pie.

"It's not apple, it's blackberry. I had no apple. It's . . . it's for you."

He did not take it at once. He just stood there looking at it. Then he looked at her. .

"Blackberry is better than apple, blackberry is— why, blackberry is heaven. Why did you do this, Selina?" He had never called her Selina before, always Miss Lockwood.

"I—I think I was sorry for a little boy."

"The little boy is grateful. The man the little boy grew into is asking you won't you still forget tomorrow?"

"And lose my inheritance?"

"And marry me," he said.

So the joke had started all over again.

"Just because of a pie," she shrugged.

"Why not? I would never consider a woman who couldn't make a pie."

It was all so ridiculous she had to laugh. He laughed too. Roger, coming up from the valley, looked over at them in astonishment.

"Roger the lodger is astounded," observed Iron slangily.

That sobered Selina. It also annoyed her.

"He is not," she said stiffly.

"Then your fiancé, Mr. Roger Peters, is taken by surprise, that ardent, reckless fiancé willing to wait three years."

Suddenly the laughter was completely dissolved between them. None from Selina. None from Iron Grant.

The man got into his car. Selina went back to the house.

Madeleine went up to Redgum Ridge every day. She drove in the Mini that Unk had given Selina for her birthday, since Selina had only ever needed it to take Unk around, so had little use for it now.

Joel had allowed Madeleine free rein with the decorations and a very generous allowance.

"He told me to do it all just as if I was doing it for myself, he had no personal preferences and no orders, which was quite a relief." Madeleine glowed. "You wouldn't recognise the place already," she told her sister.

"I wouldn't have, anyway."

"But you've been there."

"Only once, and I never looked around. I didn't want to go. I disliked him. I still do now."

"So does Roger, which is only to be expected when you two are to be one one day. You would naturally be supposed to have the same tastes and all that," Madeleine said a little sharply. "Personally I like the man," she finished.

Selina nodded, but repeated her own and Roger's dislike. "So long as they don't come to blows," she sighed.

"Who?"

"The two men, of course."

"Oh, don't be absurd!"

"You don't understand, Maddie, you only understand the city male. Tempers flare high away from concrete pavements, and these two people are very different from each other."

"If you're referring to our couple of bosses—"

"I'm referring to Roger and Iron Grant. Roger is scarcely a boss," Selina said resentfully.

"Then," continued Madeleine, ignoring her sister's interruption, "you need have no fear. I know Roger . . . I really mean I know men like Roger, Academy men, campus men, they never flare up, they're too controlled, too well trained." Madeleine was talking very quickly, she seemed annoyed with herself for some reason, and Selina wondered why.

"Well," Selina said, "I wouldn't say that about the other one."

"Joel?"

"Yes."

"Perhaps not, but he'd be strictly fair."

"You seem to know that kind of man as well," Selina observed.

"Darling, I know all men," Madeleine smiled.

Selina had not been talking idly when she had

spoken about smouldering tempers. There was an atmosphere in the air, there had been all the week, Selina could feel it very strongly. She felt sure that not all the things that Roger did pleased Iron Grant. Being Grant, he would not put up with it too long. Certainly not as long as Uncle Claud had. And can I, despaired Selina at times, put up with it all myself for three years?

She gave long thoughts to those three years. Apart from feeling . . . well, piqued, for every woman wants to be rushed, grabbed off her feet, she felt—uncertain. Not uncertain about Roger. Somewhere deep inside her, Selina knew that a hundred thousand was sufficient, and more than sufficient, to tie up Roger, but uncertain about Iron Grant. Roger had declared that the man would be ready to sell then, but would he, and if he was ready would he sell to them? At times, too, it came distastefully but very surely to Selina that no sale might not comprise such a tragedy to Roger after all, that a hundred thousand in money but no Tall Tops would not cast Roger down as it would her, that given the choice of the two—

But she put *that* thought aside.

Ignace was coming to school every day now, behaving nicely, trying hard to pick up words and often surprising and delighting Selina with a full and lucid phrase.

"Darling, that was very clever," she praised once of a good effort.

"Yes, Mummy," he said . . . and Selina turned away to hide her tears. He was a fine little boy, and he would make a fine man . . . but, Selina thought achingly, his parents would never know. However, his stepfather would, a loving stepfather, and that at least helped.

At the end of the week what Selina had felt in the air became actuality. There was a first-class row over the planting. Iron Grant believed as Unk had believed that seedlings must have room. He said so to Roger.

"But damn it all, they don't naturally," objected the overseer. "They grow up willy-nilly in the forest and survive very well, thank you."

"Only *after* they've killed off their weaklings. Yes, that's so. The forest that you encounter is a curtailed forest, Peters, curtailed beforehand by nature. If two trees are too close, one is allowed to perish. We don't do it that way. Instead we don't plant too close in the start."

"I have had success and have increased productivity," stuck out Roger.

"But not quality."

"I can't see it," Roger insisted.

"You don't have to, do you? You don't have to deal with the finished article." Iron Grant strode off.

Roger had been enraged but still controlled; Madeleine had been right when she had said that about trained men. But he still complained to Selina. He said: "I don't know if I can stand him."

"The sleeper cutter?"

"Of course."

"Then *don't*, Roger."

Roger had met Selina's eyes, read what she was thinking, asking . . . begging.

For something tight seemed to be enclosing Selina.

99

She felt if she didn't break away now, she would never break away. Break away from what? She could not have answered that. She knew she did not know, not sensibly, herself.

"Darling," Roger, recovered now, placated, "it's all nothing really, I mean we can put up with it."

"Well, I can't. Oh, Roger, can't you see—"

"I can see it would be foolish to throw away a hundred thousand dollars in a moment of pique," Roger said practically.

"It's not a moment, and it's not pique, not for me."

"Selina, you're becoming obsessed with the man, obsessed with hate."

She did not reply. She knew suddenly and sharply why there was an urgency inside her. She knew she *was* obsessed.

. . . But—was it hate?

Soon after that the big blow-up that Selina had dreaded occurred. Voices were raised in the valley, and everyone from the cook to the man who fed the mill could not help but hear. Certainly Selina heard.

"I will not," shouted Iron Grant, "*not*, mark you, Peters, have my trees cut like that!"

"They're down, aren't they?" It was Roger. "Down in half the time."

"So are four other trees."

"Not important ones."

"*I* decide on that, not you. What do you think you're playing at, ninepins? The valley looks like the aftermath of a storm!"

"Mr. Grant, in these days of time and motion—"

"More time, please, and less motion. To me a tree

is life, and I will not have my lives thrown away like that. Do you understand?"

"Well, if it means that much to you—"

"It damn well means that much to me, and if it ever happens again you can pack your bags. All twenty of them!"

That was going too far, Selina thought, surely Roger would do something now. But Roger didn't.

Selina heard the Bentley spark up, then leave Tall Tops for Redgum Ridge as though fired by a rocket. She did not know how she felt. She sympathised with Joel about the ninepins method of cutting, that cutting of several trees so that they fell on several more all down the valley, but she did not approve of his bad-tempered attack. After all, there were many who still followed the ninepins way, small foresters did, men who could only afford to employ a few hands, and Roger could have been right, the trees that had not been marked but had still fallen with the others could have been less than special. Nonetheless Uncle had disliked it. She disliked it. But most of all she disliked Joel's biting attack . . . that final sarcastic: ". . . you can pack your bags. All twenty of them!"

That had been hitting below the belt. It made a fop of Roger, and he was never that, he was simply fastidious, proud of himself as any decent male should be proud. Trust that savage to seize on such a point.

Poor Roger! She got up spontaneously and ran across to the overseer's villa to comfort him. But someone was already there.

She remembered now that Madeleine had come home early today. In the row that everyone must have heard, from the cook to the boiler feeder . . . and Madeleine . . . she had forgotten her sister.

Madeleine was sitting in Roger's lounge, Selina saw her through the window, not near Roger, in fact right across the room from him, but—yet—

Selina went back to Tall Tops again.

CHAPTER EIGHT

FOR all their differences in opinion as to how afforestation should function, their beliefs in opposite methods as to milling, transport, marketing, the two men, if not enthusiastic friends, still saw eye to eye in many important things, and grudgingly but efficiently co-operated.

"It's like the Navy and the Army in a way," trilled Madeleine, "each taking different paths but both going in the same direction."

"Marching to a different drummer," Selina put it.

The small railway lines that Roger was putting down in Tall Tops valley to meet the already established Redgum Ridge lines were proceeding satisfactorily. Roger estimated that very soon their sawdust mountain would be scarcely a tiny pimple, instead it would be on the other side of the ledge filling up a scar where Iron Grant eventually intended to establish his formal eucalyptus distillery. The distillery was working now, but the yield had proved so profitable that Grant considered it worthy of something better than the makeshift room that presently housed it. He could see it as Number One Dollar Maker, he said, and as such must be afforded every consideration.

"We'll have to stage a grand opening the first day that Billy runs up the mountain," proposed Selina one day to Madeleine.

"But it's already planned, darling," said Madeleine.

"Joel has even ordered the champagne."

"Champagne?"

"Pop for the small fry. We're going to have oodles of ribbons and I'm going to cut the ribbons, then the train will give its first toot and push up to the top."

This was news to Selina, and she felt a little put out. Why hadn't she been consulted, and why should Madeleine cut the ribbon?

Madeleine must have seen a look on her sister's face, for she added placatingly: "Being the senior, dear."

It was the first time, Selina thought, that Maddie had been anxious to be the elder. She still felt piqued. After all, it was her home ... No, no, it wasn't any more, it was his, instead she had, or would have in three years' time, a large sum of money. Money that would buy back Tall Tops. Or would it? She often asked herself that, but she never found herself an answer.

Ignace attended the verandah school every day now and was picking up quite a few words. So far they were mostly wrong words, words that sent the children into peals of laughter. At first Selina had been alarmed that the little boy would be hurt and run and hide in the bushes again, but Ignace quite enjoyed being a clown, and often, or so Selina suspected, pretended not to understand when he understood perfectly just to get the laughs.

Madeleine gave no indication of leaving for the city again. She was obviously enjoying her job of decorating up at Redgum Ridge.

"It's very satisfactory being right on the ledge," she

said to Selina, "all those pinnacled mountains beneath you, those steep-walled gorges. You really feel on the top of the world." It was totally unlike Madeleine to talk like this; secretly Selina was surprised her sister had even noticed the scenery. Maddie must be changing, she decided.

"I prefer down here," Selina said, and she meant it. Tall Tops was tall enough for her . . . and it was nearer the valleys. She loved the valleys.

She took the children down often in the pretence that it was for nature study, but actually it was to delight in the trees, especially the trees in the twilight jungle, that deepest valley of all where the sun never reached. Here, the little ones walked quietly, without being told to, for somehow they sensed that no one ran and shouted in the twilight jungle, that instead one spoke in whispers and looked with awe at the old myrtles, the old, old musks and blackwoods almost mummified in that cold corridor between the high gorges. Because it was always near-dark there, the toadstools, growing out of mouldering boles of long dead trees, gave out an electric green light. Moss encrustations and lichens were bewhiskered in silver and jade.

Although they all loved it, coming up again to the higher valleys was like casting off a spell. Now the children would shout, pretend they were Tarzans speeding through the trees, the more daring ones swinging on thick liana coils from one branch to another.

Today their joy was complete. Among the ringbarks waiting to fall, for a forest had to be disciplined otherwise it would choke, they stumbled on a carpet snake. Being timber children, they recognised the huge fellow at once, and stood gloating over his yards and yards of patterned body.

"Three dollars a foot," called Michael.

"It's gone up since inflation," said Phyllida.

Ignace, who had been looking a little doubtfully at it, came and stood by Selina's side, and she tried to tell him by words, gesticulations and drawings on the earth that this snake was a good snake, you could touch him, but you must not do such a thing with another snake.

Michael meanwhile was organising a gang to get the snake up to the chalets where they might do a deal with the storeman at three dollars a foot, even more because of inflation, because storemen liked carpet snakes around to keep down rats.

"He's terribly heavy," said Phyllida, trying the tail.

At that moment Iron Grant came down the track, saw the carpet, and gave it a goodnatured kick.

"You're taking all the sun, Eustace, get back to where you belong."

"Where is that?" asked Selina, getting into step beside Joel, and laughing as the children followed the yards of big snake who was actually proceeding obediently up the hill.

"Brent's piggery and chicken run. Eustace belongs there. They call him Eustace because it means rich in corn, which they reckon he must be, since something round there consumes more than the livestock, and it must be Eustace."

The children and the snake were out of sight now. Selina and Joel walked past marked trees that always made Selina a little sad, then finally reached Anton's totem tree, his tribute to his dead wife's and his stepson's Poland.

"Svantovit," said Selina, "He Who Can See the Whole World. Why," and she stood on tiptoe, "Anton has put a horn in his hand!"

"*I* have," claimed Joel, "and filled it with the appropriate vintage." He stepped across and lifted Selina off her feet to peer into the liquid. Ruby red. Selina put her finger in it and tasted.

"Yes, it's wine."

"What else did you think? As a matter of fact it's a very good wine. I had to make sure of that fruitfulness."

"Does the quality matter?" She was still up in the air.

"I think it might help." He made no attempt to put her down.

A little embarrassed, Selina put a finger towards the horn again.

"No," he denied, "you're supposed to help the fruitfulness, not deplete it."

"How could I help?" she asked.

"Isn't your very name fruitfulness, oh, woman?"

"Be serious!" she laughed.

"I've never been more serious in my life," he said. He put her down at last.

They walked in silence for a while. A little angrily Selina was thinking: He says this nonsense, but he gives Madeleine the ribbon-cutting honour.

"You're having a grand opening for Puffing Billy, I hear," she said coolly.

"Yes, something to mark the occasion."

"My sister is cutting the ribbon."

"Seeing that the train will be travelling up to the plateau where she's been working so well, I thought that was only fair."

"Also she's the elder, of course." Selina did not mean to snap.

"Hi, what is this? You didn't want to hold the scissors yourself, did you?"

If I was holding them right now, Selina fumed, I'd—I'd—

"We've decided on the approaching ledge gymkhana for our grand opening," Iron advised. "It's down for next week, which suits us very well. We can all proceed from Billy to the doings, which, as always, will be attracting the district boys with the axe and saw contests, not forgetting the time-honoured tug-of-war. You'll be there, of course."

"I generally go," said Selina coolly again.

He chose to ignore her frigid note.

"This time it will be history, you'll go by train instead of truck or car. Puffing Billy expects a very busy morning."

". . . After the ribbon has been cut."

He stopped, and stopped her with him.

"Are you sore about that?" he asked.

"Of course not . . . I mean—"

"I gave the job to Madeleine simply because the train is going up there" . . . he pointed . . . "and up there is her place. You're here and here is your place."

. . . Is it? Is it my place? For how long? Selina turned away.

But at once he was turning her back, turning her quite roughly.

"You tasted the wine," he reminded her a little

hoarsely, "so you can't back out."

"Back out? What on earth are you talking about, Mr. Grant?"

"I'm talking of Madeleine up there . . . but you here. *Here* . . . I repeat myself . . . *is your place*. You are committed to it."

"By tasting wine?" She laughed scornfully at him. "Is it a magic wine?" she asked.

"It's the wine of life and this is your life. I told you before."

"I remember." She made herself laugh scornfully again. "Isn't your very name fruitfulness, oh, woman?"

"Well, *isn't* it?" he asked, and his eyes were suddenly dark on her, dark and warm.

"Oh, really, Mr. Grant, this is going too far," she said.

"As a matter of fact it hasn't even started, Selina."

"Miss Lockwood."

"Does he call you that?"

"My fiancé?"

"I see by that answer that he doesn't." A deliberate pause. "And Madeleine, what does he call her?"

"I don't understand you."

Iron did not comment on that, but he gave a low laugh. The laugh followed Selina up to the house, where she finished putting the correspondence lessons that had been done this morning into their envelopes ready to be mailed.

The approaching ledge gymkhana was one of the many gymkhanas staged throughout the timberland at this time of the year. Usually the word gymkhana conjured up the idea of pony clubs, but horses were the one thing you did not get at these outdoor offerings, not, anyway, the timberland variety. The emphasis was on men, not horses.

On the arranged Saturday of the ledge gymkhana, so Selina read in the pamphlet that came up with the mail from the road box, there would be the time-honoured tree felling, log cutting, sawing, and, as was always the case, the tug-of-war. Timber men loved a tug-of-war.

Like the axemen and the sawyers, they would travel long distances to participate. Last year Western Australia had travelled across, and, as Unk had said, three states and a continent's entire width was a very long way to come to pull a piece of rope.

Madeleine was getting quite excited over her ribbon-cutting role that took place before the gymkhana so that the Puffing Billy travellers would have ample time to make it to the field. She had even gone down to Tallow Wood to buy a ribbon-cutting dress, as she gaily put it, and had come back saying that country styles weren't so bad after all, and had displayed a turquoise silk creation that promised to do wonderful things for her already wonderful eyes.

Just to be unco-operative, Selina purchased nothing. She was still smarting over the fact that Madeleine, newly returned, should have taken precedence when it came to signalling the small train off for its initial ascent from Tall Tops. It was all very well for Iron Grant to say that up there was Maddie's place, here was her place, but the fact remained that she had been around Tall Tops all her life, she had never left here, so shouldn't she have been given the honour?

So, on the Saturday morning of the function,

Selina put on her navy knife-pleated skirt and her white blouse, and looked, she knew without Madeleine telling her, like the prefect of the class.

She was sorry, when she reached the clearing and saw all the other Tall Tops people in their gayest and brightest, and Puffing Billy fairly smothered with balloons and ribbons, that she had been so stubborn. Glancing across to Joel Grant, actually wearing a frivolous rosette in his shirt, she saw that he was displeased as well.

Jock, seated at the controls of Billy and dressed up also, at a nod from the boss started the engine, then diminished it to the lowest tick possible so that Madeleine could be heard in her part of the performance. Madeleine said inappropriately but to much laughter: "I name you Billy, and may God bless you and all who sail in you." She added charmingly: "Oh, dear, that isn't quite right, is it?"

No one cared, for the bottle of champagne Maddie had released had spilled over Billy, but other champagne was being produced, and pop for the small ones.

Then in the middle of it all, Jock pressed the tooter, and Iron Grant turned round and bowed low and gallantly to Selina.

"Me?" She knew she could not be heard above the cheers and shouts, but all at once Joel Grant was so close he had to hear her.

"Who else?" he asked. "Gym-slip and all."

"It isn't a gym-slip!"

"You could have fooled me."

"If I'd known—"

"It wouldn't have been a surprise. Please get in,

Miss Lockwood, we're ready to go."

She got in, completely mollified, saying foolishly it was a pity such immaculate polish would by next week be marred by wet sawdust, for it would have to be damped down not to fly away.

He did not answer, and she looked where he was looking, and was silent, too. She had thought she had known Tall Tops, but now, travelling vertically, she saw things she had never seen before. Deep gorges and chasms and small peaks standing out in symmetrical beauty, water hurtling from suddenly abrupt places she had not even known were there. Trees everywhere.

Instinctively her hand was dropping down to his and he was holding it. Hand in hand they went up the mountain right to the sky—at least that was how it felt.

They joined the old line at Redgum Ridge and continued up to the ledge. Jock returned at once in Billy to fetch a second load. He reckoned it would take him an hour to bring all Tall Tops to the top. "There's not anyone," he called cheerfully as he started back, "travelling by car today."

Selina and Joel waited until Madeleine and Roger ascended, then the four of them strolled off to the gymkhana grounds. Considering that the ledge . . . everyone called it the ledge . . . was edged by deep valleys on four sides and was really only an unexpected pasture on the top of a minor plateau that could only be reached by small aircraft or rough track (in Tall Tops' and Redgum Ridge's instances today by Puffing Billy) there was a remarkable attendance.

Tallow Wood teams had flown in by special helicopter shuttle service, and there were several Cessnas that had brought in interstate sawyers and axemen, since, although the location was remote, the prestige here was high.

The fun of the fair already had begun. Little marquees had been erected, a tea tent, a fortune-telling tent, a beer tent and a lemonade tent rigged up. There was no need for any changing tent, the competitors came as they always came, in white pants, black singlet and white boots, ready for the starter's signal. Meanwhile a chocolate wheel rattled, trying to gather money for future gymkhanas, and the grass became noticeably thinner and littered with lolly wrappers.

At noon, when the committee decided that everyone who intended coming had come, the whistle blew for the first event. The Single-handed Championship Saw. There were six sawyers competing, though eight logs had been set up. Selina listened to the usual instructions she had known from a child, as to three blocks to be severed and all saw cuts to be started as close as possible to the front end of the log.

She heard: "Sawyers, stand by your logs." Then she saw to her utter surprise, no surprise over Iron, for it was the kind of thing he would do, but surprise at—Roger.

Roger stood by a log. He must have intended to enter, just as Iron must have intended, for both the men now wore white pants, black athletic singlets and white boots like the rest of the squad. They must have had them on under their outer clothes ready for this moment. But Roger's gear looked entirely different from the rest. Even in something like sawing a log, Roger had to be impeccable. There was not a pucker anywhere and his slacks were immaculately creased.

"He won't know anything about it," Selina fretted unhappily to herself. She did not want Roger to be embarrassed.

Madeleine, who had come to stand near her, gave a short laugh.

"Oh, Roger knows."

"How can you say that?" Selina asked in surprise; several times Madeleine had spoken as though she was more aware of Roger than was thought.

"The Academy," Madeleine said impatiently, actually impatient with herself and her too-ready tongue had Selina looked at her. "They go in for the scientific side, but that does not mean that they don't know the other side as well."

"But how would you know, Maddie?"

"Oh, I don't. Not really. But even a full-fledged chef once must have boiled potatoes. In other words, an afforestation graduate must have learned how to chop or saw a tree as well. But stop chattering, Selina. It's beginning."

It was. The starter was intoning: "Get ready—set —go!"

And it was on.

Almost before they realised the entire line of men were halfway through their first logs. Some worked like Puffing Billy, putting everything into it, some were naturally quicksilver, some appeared effortless, some seemed to wield the saw to a rhythm.

Iron and Roger were not, Selina was relieved to observe, the tortoises in the line. But neither were they the hares, who by this time were on their second logs.

The dead silence that had dropped with the starter's 'Get ready' was breaking up now. The people were beginning to get excited. As everyone favours an underdog, the spectators were shouting for the tortoise of the sawyers, who was steadily but surely catching up ground. By the time the third log was reached the tortoise passed the leader, and one moment later it was all over, with a second, third, fourth, then after that, the judge announced, the rest stood at dead level.

Selina saw Iron Grant look across to Roger and call: "Quits, Peters. I'll double up that wager in the cut."

"Done," Roger called back.

So they were betting on themselves.

The cut was always the more thrilling event. No one ever could see an underhand cut and not stand fascinated.

All the big names were here today, Crawford, the current Sydney Royal axeman, Tulloch from Tasmania, Smith from Gippsland where the trees reached four hundred feet. Joel Grant. Roger Peters. They were all tall, and they all wore the black singlets cut deeply under the arm to allow free movement for rippling muscles.

"I never," Selina murmured, "thought Roger had muscles."

"Of course," Madeleine said. "He'd have to, leading an outdoor life."

It was still a surprise to Selina . . . but Iron Grant was no surprise. There he stood, a little taller but a lot broader than the others, and Red Indian to their brown. She wished she could look away from him, but every time she tried she found herself looking back.

The men were squinting at their axes, gleaming

silver axes, most of them imported from the States, for the best racing axes came from America. Selina heard the starter, and again it was on.

The same as the tortoise in the sawing, a second tortoise, actually Crawford who had won the Sydney Royal, played Wait-and-See with the axe boys. He was behind all the way, then suddenly he was in front, his axe flailing through the air like a machine. Then his log was severed. The second, third and fourth were announced, then, the same as with the saw event, the rest categorised as dead level.

This time it was Roger who looked across and issued a challenge.

"But what else can they bet on?" said Madeleine.

"The tug-of-war," groaned Selina.

"But this is all too silly. Surely those two men aren't going to pull against each other at the end of a rope?"

"No, but Tall Tops has a team, it always has, and I expect Redgum Ridge has one, too. The men will be coaching their respective sides."

As she said it, Tall Tops' eight men were taking their place on the rope . . . Anton Wolhar was one of them, and Ignace was jumping up and down with excitement. Roger came and stood beside his team.

Iron Grant brought his boys out, then that favourite recreation of all for mountain men began, that heave back, that resistance to the opponent's heave, that careful strategy, those words of advice from the coach. That best out of three pulls.

The first pull took only seconds. **Tall Tops** took Redgum Ridge by surprise and had them over the line soon after they had started. The second pull went the same way, only to Joel Grant this time. The third pull reached into minutes, and at last was called off as an equal win because the professional teams were waiting for their turn.

"Redgum Ridge and Tall Tops dead level," called the announcer, and everyone clapped . . . except Roger and Iron, who looked across at each other and this time made no wager. One of the Redgum Ridge men, who had come to watch beside Selina, told her disgustedly that the boss wasn't trying.

"But he wasn't pulling, Harry."

"I don't mean the team events, I mean the individual saw and cut, especially the cut. If Iron had wanted to win, he would have brought his Philadelphia axe with him. And I put ten dollars on the boss."

"He still mightn't have won," said Selina.

"There's no one could beat Iron and that Yankee axe."

The rest of the day went like all gymkhanas did. Tea in the tea tent for the ladies, the men in the beer tent, the kids round the cake and pop.

Madeleine and Selina patronised the fortune-teller, who told Selina the same as she had last year, and years before that. The grass grew thinner and more scattered with lolly wrappers. Joel Grant announced through the loudspeaker that the new T.T. train was returning its passengers from four o'clock onward, and the Tall Toppers began moving away.

Selina had been the first to come up on Billy, but something decided her not to complete the circle by being the last one to leave. It was the sight of Madeleine, Madeleine with an arm in an arm of each of the two men. Roger and Joel. They were looking at her as men did look at Madeleine, and Selina turned quickly, left the fair and hurried across to the landing platform.

Had it only been a sawing contest Roger and Iron had been competing in? she was suddenly wondering. An axe cut? A length of rope?

From the way they both had looked at Madeleine just now a woman came into it, too, a lovely woman with blue eyes and copper hair.

"Fezplis," called Ignace, well pleased with these new words he had learned today from driver Jock who had chosen him for his conductor. "Fezplis," and Selina took out five cents and gave it to the little boy.

How foolish I am, she thought, I am like Anton's Svantovit, looking from all quarters. Seeing too much.

CHAPTER NINE

THE following week saw a big change in Puffing Billy. Stripped of his balloons and streamers the morning following the gymkhana, he steadily lost his glamour to become a working engine instead. It was remarkable what wet sawdust could do to a spit and polish train . . . yet even more remarkable what a train could do to sawdust. In no time their sawdust mountain was the pimple Roger had spoken about, and soon even the pimple was gone. There were still twenty tons to account for daily, but Billy took the tons in his stride, or at least on his back, up the vertical track. He also took logs, mill pieces, machinery, brought back tools, food for Brent's piggery and chickens, exchange equipment from Redgum . . . and one morning, instead of in his Bentley, Joel Grant.

Iron strode up from the clearing, but paused on the way to the house at the totem tree to inspect the horn of wine.

"Still there?" he called to Selina, who was out on the verandah, and who could not pretend she had not seen him and duck inside since he had previously waved to her.

"What else did you expect?" she asked.

"Well, no noticeable evaporation as yet, but I did fear a little human interference."

"No one knows about the wine."

"You do."

"If you think—" she began.

"Oh, I think all right. I saw that pilfering finger the other day. This finger, wasn't it? Or this?" He had reached the house and climbed the steps by now. He had her hand in his and was considering the fingers in turn. She wondered if he was noticing the difference between her hands and Madeleine's, Maddie's so silky, so white, the nails so long, so tapered, so tended and so red. Her own hand was quite square, a good commonsense hand, the nails cut straight except where she sometimes nibbled at the first finger on the left hand.

Iron did notice. He noticed the shorter nail.

"So you've been helping yourself," he accused, "while climbing up the totem tree you lost some of this nail."

"I didn't!" she snapped.

"You kept the nail, then? Or preserved it in Svantovit's wine?"

"Oh, don't be ridiculous! I bit it. I do upon occasions when I'm—"

"Yes? When you're—?"

"It's of no interest."

"I find it quite interesting. Usually nail-nibblers are emotional people I would never have thought it of you." He was regarding her with mock intrigue.

"Did you come for something, Mr Grant?" she asked politely.

"Yes, to see you."

"You are seeing me."

"I should have said to speak to you, and don't come back that I'm already speaking to you, because I'm not. That's just exchange of words. Please ask me in, put on the billy, then we'll discuss a few things."

Selina did as she was bid, it was the easiest way with this man, then brought the tea things to the office where he had now settled himself. Well, why not? It was his office.

She poured and passed, and he accepted and drank, after which he said with the usual Grant lack of preamble: "I wish to discuss your pay."

"My what?"

"I said pay, because I don't know whether you come under Wages or Salaries."

"I don't understand what you're talking about."

"You're teaching my kids, aren't you?"

"I'm supervising the correspondence lessons of the children of Tall Tops, yes," she agreed.

"Same thing. Well, I always pay for services rendered."

"But I'm being paid now—I mean, I'm staying in a house that isn't mine."

"You would have to stay on to do any supervising regardless, wouldn't you? You could scarcely travel up and down from Tallow Wood every day."

"You did suggest a room in the overseer's villa," she dared.

"I changed my mind about that." At her raised brows, he added: "A privilege, surely, of the boss of the outfit." When she did not comment he went on: "However, I am talking of *payment*, Miss Lockwood, not fringe benefits."

"Living here is payment in kind."

"Not my kind."

"My uncle's kind, then."

"Nor his, either."

"He never paid me," Selina pointed out.

"Then how has he left you all that money?"

"You bought the property from him." She could not keep a bitter note from her voice. Why had Uncle Claud done what he had?

"Yes, but how did the property get that good? It was because Claud ploughed into it the wages he knew you wouldn't take from him. It made a better place of it. Money always does that, along, of course, with hard work. But it's a different story with me. You'll take—" He named a sum that widened her eyes.

"That's generous," she commented.

"I'm a generous fellow." He had pushed his empty cup aside and was lighting his pipe. The scratch of the lighter flint made the only noise in an otherwise silent room in a silent house. Selina thought she had never known the house so silent before. She saw the flame of the lighter, the man's face behind the flame, that red brown skin of a man who has lived all his life out of doors, she saw the eyes narrowed above the flame. Narrowed at her.

She looked away. He waited a moment, then he said: "Here is your first pay envelope, Miss Lockwood. I suggest a few dresses, that prefect's gym outfit you wore to the gymkhana hardly made the pulses flutter."

"It wasn't intended to."

"Not even the good Roger's?"

"Roger isn't like that," Selina said coldly.

"My dear child, all men are like that."

She put the pay envelope down on the desk. "If this comes with a stipulation on how it's to be spent

122

I'd sooner not take it."

"You'll take it all right and no doubt put it in the bank. After all, you don't know what I'm going to charge you, do you, in three years?"

She looked at him incredulously, and he nodded calmly back.

"I know what you're planning in your cunning little mind, how wouldn't I know?"

"Roger told you?"

"He certainly did not. Anyway, he wouldn't be sufficiently interested to do so."

"Roger is terribly interested, he loves Tall Tops like I do."

"But" . . . the brows raised quizzically . . . "the cash would do equally well?"

There were so many things she wanted to retort that none managed to come. It was usually like that. Instead she said: "Then Madeleine told you. You certainly see enough of her for her to tell."

"Yes to the second, no to the first. I do see a lot of Madeleine, but Madeleine did not tell. I gathered it on my own accord. Gathered it from your eyes, your lips, the whole of you, from everything you do and are. You and this place are one."

"So?" she challenged.

"So you put aside every penny to bargain with me in three years' time. 'Mr Grant', you will say, 'I offer you—' "

"And what does" . . . Selina breathed very hard . . . "Mr. Grant say in return?"

"Ah, that's the sixty-four-dollar question, isn't it, something that time alone will tell. Do you think I can have some more tea?"

Selina did go down to Tallow Wood to buy a few frocks, but that was because she needed them, not because she had said that skirts and blouses don't make the pulses flutter. She also made a substantial bank deposit, thinking ruefully that had he been there he could have taken a bow on both accounts.

Coming out of the bank she became aware, as you do become aware sometimes, and especially in a small place, of someone watching her. She glanced curiously across and saw an oldish middle-aged man looking at her. He looked away at once, but not before she had registered shabbiness . . . and a kind of wistfulness. Wistful for what? She wondered if the fellow was hard up. In Uncle's days she would have taken him up to Tall Tops with her, found him a niche some-where. He didn't look very robust, but there was a lot of work at a lumber camp as well as hard physical work. He could help Cooky, or if he was the bookish type assist Mr. Brown with the wages and accounts.

However, Uncle was not boss any more, and she had not the right to return with a new employee. Besides, it might not have been a good move, these days all kinds of dubious people were on the road. Though—and she glanced over again—he didn't look harmful.

She finished her shopping and set off for the moun-tains. It did not take her long to leave the township behind, after that the crumpled blue-green grass of the foothills, and then she was into the sharp turn and the steep rises of the Tall Tops ascent.

No opportunity now to look at gushy streams, at trees full of parrots, at ferns and mosses and trails of wild orchids, the road from Tallow Wood took up every moment of a driver's attention. Selina knew it well, though, knew it by its many names marking its many bends. Rogue's Corner ... Dead Horse Rise ... Roaring Jimmy ... of all tags, Piccadilly Circus.

It was just beyond Piccadilly Circus and ... fortunately as it happened ... just before the old and now disused track up to Tall Tops when she turned with the contour of the mountain and saw the car. That meant nothing, it was a public road, and though cars were not plentiful they certainly were not rare. But the position of this car was rare. It was right over the road, blocking anyone coming or going, and meaning that if she was to pass she would have to call out to the driver to correct his own vehicle first. But the car was empty and there was no driver in sight.

She was still proceeding, but very slowly now, trying to work out what was the best thing to do. She was fully conscious of the possible danger in the situation; she was inexperienced, but she was not naïve. The fact that there was no one in the car, no one in sight, alerted her. She could alight only to find out that her alighting had been expected, that it had been planned that way, and that someone was lying in wait either for her, or for her car, so that to step from the Mini might be a very foolish move.

She had fifty more yards to go, but between the car and where she was moving now almost at snail's pace was the old turn-off. Probably the now discarded road was in a bad state, overgrown in many places, but she did not think it would be unmanoeuvrable. Bumpy and unpleasant driving perhaps, very bad for tyres, but not impossible.

Thirty yards to go. Twenty. Still no driver, still no one anywhere. Ten. Selina turned her car down the old track.

Right from the first moment she detoured she was appalled at the growth that had taken place since the new road had been in use. Young saplings had sprung up in the most inconvenient spots, and branches of larger trees scraped the sides of the car and at times seemed as though they would stop her altogether. But by proceeding gently but firmly, she was able to get through, though she shuddered to think how the duco must be faring.

It was getting dark. That was understandable, she had left Tallow Wood in the late afternoon, and the blockage on the road had frittered away a lot of time, while the negotiation of the old track, even this short distance of the old track, must have eaten up over an hour. Still, it was a more direct way than the new road, so with the same fair luck as she was having now she should reach Tall Tops before it was actual night.

She inched carefully round a bend and said: "Oh, no!"

Across the path, just as the car had been across the road from Tallow Wood, was a very large log.

Selina looked at it in dismay. She knew there was nothing, just nothing, she could do. A log that size would stay there until it mouldered away in, say, ten years. She felt for a miserable minute like mouldering away herself. It was too far to walk to Tall Tops. It was too far now to walk back to the Tallow Wood road. There was nothing else for it but to sit. Sit all night.

Because she never went driving at night, not up here, Selina had no rug in the car. No cushion. No biscuits. And . . . looking estimatingly at the semi-gloom . . . it could not be much more than seven.

It was going to be a very long evening.

She closed the windows and leaned back. She tried to assure herself that a rest would do her good.

But it was difficult to rest in an Australian forest, there were too many noises, a scrape and slither of leaves and twigs as a small animal or a snake pushed through, the plop of a fallen leaf, the drip somewhere of water. A mopoke.

. . . And behind her, coming slowly as it would have to come, another car.

Selina sat petrified. Then, with difficulty, she made herself turn the handle of the door. Before the car came and found its way blocked by her car, she had to be out of her car and concealed somewhere. She did not know whether it was the car on the Tallow Wood road that was behind her, whether it was following her, but she had no intention of waiting to find out.

She wrenched at the door, in her agitation not twisting the handle properly. Then when she did twist it, and open up, she made the mistake of slamming the door shut again, which would mean she would have to run so much harder because he, whoever was in the following car, would hear the bang. But she couldn't run. Her dress was caught. She went through the terrifying business of trying to release herself in a hurry . . . and was picked up by a spotlight.

She stood in the spotlight, not knowing which way to turn, and when at last she made up her mind, and turned left, she turned into imprisoning arms. The spotlight was still fixed, he must have left it like that, but she was fixed, too, fixed by those imprisoning arms, she could not move an inch.

"Help!" she sobbed into some material. She knew she could not be heard, but she cried it all the same.

"Yes, little one? What kind of help was it you required?" Iron Grant's voice came patronisingly down to her, and Selina knew relief and apprehension in the same breath. Relief that there was no danger, apprehension as to what would come next.

Actually he seated her back in the car next. But before he did he brought a rug, a pillow and a flask from the car behind. He made her comfortable, poured some coffee, waited till she drank it, before he spoke.

Then he said, drawing in a long hard breath: "What in tarnation do you think you're at?"

"Nothing. Nothing at all. There was a car blocking the Tallow Wood road and I wasn't taking any risk."

"Very prudent of you, except, you young idiot, that it was mine."

"Yours? It wasn't your Bentley."

"I use the Holden for lesser occasions. You must have seen it before."

Yes, she had seen it, in fact she had seen it quite often, but she must have forgotten. Anyway, it was a common make and a popular colour, one you would encounter anywhere, so how would she have known it was his, especially with the number out of sight with the car positioned like that?

"I didn't position it," he said irritably, "skidded. I only went down the valley a minute, no more, to get a few big stones, and when I struggle back I see you turning down the old track."

"You knew my car?"

"Of course. I'm not like you, madam. I also recognised the stupidity you generally succeed in demonstrating."

"You're unfair! Did you want me to stop and be killed?"

"I wouldn't have killed you," he said drily, "but I think at least you could have stayed in the Mini, winding up the windows, of course, and waited at least to make sure that someone else wasn't hurt or killed."

"I never thought," she admitted.

"No," he agreed, "but think now."

She did, and was a little ashamed of herself.

"I suppose it was that man," she murmured.

"What man?"

"A stranger in Tallow Wood. He kept on looking at me."

"Why? Were you looking at him?"

"No. He was old. Well—oldish middle-aged. Very shabby and—and wistful somehow."

"So you looked sympathetically at him and he consequently tagged on after you departed. That was what you were thinking?"

"In a way."

"Then how in Betsy would he get in *front* of you?" Joel Grant asked, exasperated.

"I didn't really think it was him. I didn't really think of anything. I just took the old track."

"And stopped. Why did you stop?" Joel focused his very powerful torch and groaned. "Now I see," he said.

"Any hope of rolling the log away?"

"*You* ask that? You, a lumber girl?"

"I suppose it is a bit big," she agreed.

"A big bit big. It would feed the mill boilers for a week. No, we're stuck here."

"We? But you're manoeuvrable. I mean, you could get out," she pointed out.

"So were you before I came behind you."

"But I felt I couldn't reverse. That car might still have been on the road."

"Well, madam, *I* am not reversing, not in this dark of evening along a track full of saplings, ruts and holes. The Holden is considerably bigger than your car, and I had enough trouble coming down."

"Then what do we do?"

"Do? We sit here, of course."

"Sit here?" she gasped.

"Sit here all night, unless you like to try to find your way on foot. Just listen to that dingo."

Selina did not listen. She was too much of an old hand to be frightened of dingoes who, anyway, would be frightened of her, but she also did not attempt to step out of the car.

"It's going to be a long night," she said again, but this time to both of them.

"Ten hours of dark at least."

"You're quite sure you couldn't——"

"I'm quite sure I couldn't."

"Then—then can I have another cup of coffee, please?"

"Half only. It's not a bottomless flask and I intend having my share." He poured her share into the flask top and handed it to her, waited till she finished, then drank his own.

"What do we do now?" he asked idly. "Play I Spy?"

"Don't be silly!"

"Well, it's a long night, as you said, Selina Lockwood, so best to keep the mind occupied, otherwise—" His voice trailed off.

A little drowsily, for the few stars she could see between the trees were starting to run into one star, Selina asked: "Otherwise?"

"You don't know?"

"What, Mr. Grant?" Very drowsily now.

"Just sleep on it, little one," he said.

Selina slept. When she woke she was folded very close to Iron Grant. She had both the pillow, the rug and his coat as well.

"You shouldn't have," she protested of the extra covering. She was still half limp with sleep.

"I wasn't cold," he told her.

"But you still shouldn't have." She glanced down at his protective arms still tight around her.

"It was no punishment." He said it a little indistinctly.

"You slept yourself?" she asked hurriedly.

"I was afraid to in case I dreamed."

"Dreamed?"

He did not answer that, instead he said: "Look it's dawn."

She blinked through the shadowy trees and saw a pale buttering in the sky. Almost at once the buttering deepened to primrose, then the first bird called.

Abruptly, with the morning, a hardness came to

the man. He was the Ridge boss, the sleeper cutter again.

"We'll get moving," he said crisply. "I'll do the reversing and you'll do the guiding. Tell me if I'm running into any trees."

"And my Mini?"

"I'll send one of the boys down for it. Now get cracking. The earlier we return the less likelihood we'll be noticed."

"Noticed?" she asked stupidly.

"That's what I said. People are the same the world over, whether the location is Paris, New York . . . or a lumber camp in the middle of nowhere."

"I don't understand you," she said.

"Then understand this," harshly. "I'm male. You're female. We are now returning at five in the morning after a night's absence. Do you see, Miss Lockwood?"

"Not really. I mean, it's so absurd."

"That's what you think?"

"Yes."

"It would be absurd with Peters?"

"Roger doesn't come into this," she said coldly.

"The man you propose to marry doesn't come into an all-night caper?"

"It was not a caper!"

"Try telling him that. Anyway, all is not lost yet, not if we get cracking as I said." To prompt her, he got out of the car and crossed back to his Holden. When he had sparked the engine, Selina sighed and got out of the Mini, then crossed to do as he said.

It did not take long to get back to the Tallow Wood road. Last night it had seemed hours and the track full of hazards. Now Iron breezed out, waited for Selina to join the car, then without speaking he drove the rest of the way to Tall Tops.

They were fortunate. No one was around. The chalets were not yet astir and the mess hut's doors were closed.

"Uncompromised by the favour of several minutes, I'd say," Joel Grant laughed. "First shift is at six, so Cooky must stoke up quite soon."

Selina did not comment on that. She got out of the car and said correctly: "Thank you."

"Of course," he continued, ignoring her courtesy, "you still have Madeleine to cope with, but I hardly think she'll make any comments. If she does there's always tit for tat."

Selina looked at him curiously, then furiously, but he stopped the look at that, at just a look.

"Next time you're in Tallow," he said firmly, evidently finished with the other subject, "please don't gather any more middle-aged pixies."

"He wasn't, and I didn't. I simply told you I saw a man ... I mean, a man looked at me, and he was shabby and had wistful eyes."

"Then leave it at that. Good night—I mean good morning, Miss Lockwood. You slept last night. I didn't. Someone had to keep the dingoes at bay." Without another word he started the Holden and was well on his private road to the Ridge by the time Selina climbed the front steps.

Madeleine came out drinking coffee. "Yes, I'm up early, Sellie. I didn't hear you come in last night."

"I was at Tallow Wood, buying dresses."

"All night?"

"There was a—an incident."

"I suppose so." Madeleine yawned. "Show me the dresses."

"They're in the Mini down in the forest."

"Oh." Madeleine looked at Selina, and Selina recalled her moment of curiosity and anger when Iron had said:

"... if she comments, there's always tit for tat."

Tit for tat?

But Madeleine did not comment. She just laughed. In another minute Selina was laughing back. They laughed ... and laughed.

It was the nearest Selina had felt to Madeleine in her life.

CHAPTER TEN

MADELEINE did not comment, either, in the days that followed. Sometimes Selina wished at least that she would ask questions, then she could ask a few back.

Tit for tat. What *had* Iron Grant meant by that?

Tall Tops was beginning a big planting project the following week. A valley had been cleared and tilled, and truckloads of boxes of tree seedlings brought up from Tallow Wood. Every worker had been assigned to the job, and men from Redgum were coming down to lend a hand.

Cooky was baking literally yards of Cut and Come Again. It really was yards, because the cake tins he put in the large range must have extended twenty-four inches at least, and as soon as one cake came out, another went in. But cake was the only prior preparation. From the very first planting years ago, the dinner had been barbecued steak, damper cooked in ashes, billy tea. Uncle would not have dreamed of changing it, and Selina was glad to find that both Roger and Joel approved. But then so had an American timber project that had started several mountains to the north. The Washington Company had been aghast at first at the wastage of time for cooking steaks and kneading dampers, until they had realised that you can't fight tradition, that it was more time-wasting again filling flasks and slicing bread . . .

most important of all that this way men worked better.

Everyone in Tall Tops and Redgum went to the planting and everyone planted. The smallest children brought their own little spades. Mindful of her own childhood, Selina provided pretty lengths of ribbon to tie to the littlies' seedlings, so they could recognise them later and remark on their growth.

"Was this your own ribbon once, Selina?" Ignace asked. Ignace could say almost anything now, he had learned very fast.

"Yes, Ignace."

"For your hair?"

"Well—yes."

"My mother wore ribbons in her hair," the little boy said.

But that was the only cloud on a perfect day, and just a small cloud that soon passed. It was perfect down in the planting valley. The children planted the smaller trees, mostly cypress, but the men attended to the bigger seedlings for large trees, inserting the root ball with assiduous care so as to set the young tree in the same depth as it had been in its pot. A depression was put around the tree to collect moisture, it was well watered, then on to the next future forest giant.

The men, of course, did not bother about identification, they had long since grown out of that, but the little ones carefully tied on their ribbons and tags, and even Ignace soon forgot to look back.

Lunch was a wonderful party. T-bones for the adults, sausages for the small fry, black billy tea and a bottle of cordial to be broken down at the waterfall only a few yards away, for the children. And damper. Dampers emerging from the ashes and being cleaned of their charcoal, then sliced and served with a slab of icy butter. Nothing else.

"There's nothing," said Iron, "*nothing* in all the world like damper."

Even the ants were beaten to the crumbs. After that it was backs-down for half an hour. Everyone stretched out, and in the heat of high noon, with the tang of the dying gum fire, the mountain sweet air, they slept.

But Selina did not sleep. She could not remember feeling so happy. Planting day was always joyous, but this was the most joyous of all, she thought with wonder. She half-closed her eyes to the burning sun and watched the few white clouds etched like fretwork through the leaves of the trees.

She was resting a little apart from the others, and she did not see Joel roll idly over and over the ground to her until he said softly:

"One cent."

"If that's for my thoughts, there's inflation."

"A dollar," he enticed.

"I was thinking of Unk, whether he's enjoyed the planting as we have today."

"If he's had time, yes," Iron said.

"Time?"

"Selina, if you could push over that tree and scatter that cloud I've no doubt you'd see old Claud driving a team of heavenly bullocks up from a felling, flattening the track with the jinker's grinding wheels, and using the usual curses."

"Curses up there?"

"Curses would be forgiven," Joel assured her, "in the lumber forests of heaven."

She loved it when he talked like that, and her eyes

must have said so. His own eyes looked back into hers, no banter, no narrowed estimation, just a man's eyes looking into a woman's.

At the end of the day Joel reported fifteen thousand seedlings accounted for, not adding the children's. It had been a most successful planting.

Madeleine drove down to Tallow Wood through the week. She was up to drapes in her decoration, and once again Joel let her have a free hand. She knew what she wanted, so it would be no advantage to have Selina accompany her, she told her sister. When she returned, though, she was not so certain. A man had followed her in Tallow Wood, she was sure of it, whichever store she had gone into, whenever she had turned, he had been there.

"Oldish middle-aged. Shabby. Kind of wistful." It was Selina.

"Well—yes. But that wistfulness could be a front."

"He didn't follow you here, though."

"A person like that would obviously not have transport, and certainly couldn't afford to pay for it. I wonder what he wanted."

"*Your* answer is easy. He would want to follow you just to admire you. But I encountered him, too, and I'm sure he wouldn't want to admire me."

Typical of Madeleine, who only ever considered herself, she did not argue this. She forgot the episode in her triumphant showing to Selina of the lengths she had tracked down in the different stores.

"I couldn't have done better in Sydney."

Selina often felt tempted to try her own hand on redecoration at Tall Tops. Only two things stopped her. One: it was not her place. Two: Tall Tops was definitely brown and marigold as to colour, chintz and cottage weave as to curtain and cushion. For that *was* Tall Tops. So she left it alone.

But she had to do something with her time, and, seeing the children only worked till noon, she decided to spend her unfilled hours on them. She took them to the pool that Iron Grant had built. It was a modern pool, looking rather like a big blue bathtub belonging to some cleanliness-is-next-to-godliness believing giant. The children loved it. They were not afraid of its clear, dancing blue water, made bluer again by its blue tile lining. There was not one of them who had not responded to the gift by not learning to swim. Even the smallest could manage a few strokes. Even Ignace, who had only been introduced to the pool a short time ago, could keep himself afloat.

There were other excursions. A trip up to the distillery to see how the precious eucalyptus oil was coaxed from the gum leaves, though the best part of that trip, Selina suspected, was the journey in Puffing Billy. It was a case of dust the seat first now in Billy.

"He's spoiled," mourned Phyllida, "he's all sawdusty and splintery, not pretty like he was before."

But they still enjoyed the trip, and Ignace remembered, and practised again, his: "Fezplis."

Then Selina took the children to the old mill. No one knew much about the old mill. Even Unk had had no tales to tell about it. It had been here even when he had arrived, and that had been very early in the piece; Uncle Claud always had boasted that he had been one, if not the first, of the beginners. But somewhere back in the nineteen-hundreds someone must have come and built a millhouse and created a mill-race. The old house had tumbled years ago, only a hearth stone remained, but the mill-race still raced. Selina explained the purpose of a race to her children, how a body of water suddenly found it could only escape through a pipe. She showed them the pool, then the pipe.

"It's remarkable," she told them, "that the pipe is still intact."

"In tacks?" asked Michael. "I can't see any tacks."

"I meant, dear, that it's still the same as when it was put down. Now shall we have our party?"

Anything out in the open accompanied by a cordial was a party. They all sat down happily. Selina had no fear that they would venture in the water. After the glimmering blue of Iron's bathtub pool how could she have fears of that? For the old millpool was, if anything, unattractive. It had a green scum, and it was enveloped with throngs of gauzy gnats. It also, though slightly, stank.

But children ... or so Selina thought at first when the thing happened ... don't see such things. Later, but too late, she discovered that children did, that they are as fastidious as grown-ups.

It all began with Ignace's cap. Because it was cool, if sunny, Anton Wolhar had put on his stepson's head a little astrakhan cap. It was a beautiful cap. Selina herself had often cast an envious eye on it, and every little girl ... and boy ... would have done a swap at once.

But Ignace did not see it like that. He saw himself very distastefully in a foreign cap when everyone else was either bareheaded or wearing a local footie beanie. He hated his cap. He left it in numerous places, but

140

every time Selina saw it and said: "Ignace, your lovely cap."

On the last occasion Ignace had complained: "It is not lovely. I hate it!" But he had still taken it up.

Now that the 'party' was over, the cake and cordial consumed and drunk, the children bickering and arguing amicably among themselves, Selina lay back and thought. She thought a lot of late. She shut her eyes for a moment ... she was sure afterwards it was only a moment ... then she opened them to no children, no children at all. But in the middle of the millpond a cap. An astrakhan cap. Ignace's cap.

Selina acted instinctively ... and foolishly. Without even calling the expected Cooee ... 'come here' ... without even shouting out for an explanation from Ignace wherever he was ... without even looking around, she jumped into the pond and swam towards the cap. It was a reckless move, if only she had waited even one second she would have realised this. What child, especially a child who hated his cap and would be glad to see the end of it, would jump into a green, rather slimy, gnat-infested, frog-loud, smelly pool? Particularly a pool with at one end of it an evil-looking race? But Selina leapt.

At first the slime, the gnats and the frog chorus enclosed her, then, coming gradually but inevitably to the pipe, where the water activity showed more ripples, it was a different story. All that Selina could relate afterwards was that one minute she was there, the next—

She saw the cap as she travelled past it. It caught up to her again in a sudden eddy from the left, then it, with Selina, disappeared from sight.

*   *   *

Selina seemed to be coming to a bright shore. Then she seemed to be withdrawing from the shore. To. Fro. To. Fro. Full of wellbeing as she thrust forward and upward one moment, feeling herself a dead leaf falling from a tree as she withdrew the next moment. Brightness. Darkness. Sweet air in her lungs. Choking in foulness. Then out of the chaos a clear pattern emerging. A face pattern. Someone's face against hers. Someone breathing into her mouth.

The withdrawal stopped. The darkness stopped. The choking stopped. She opened her eyes and looked at Joel Grant and he said: "Thank God!"

That was all he said for almost ten minutes. He had banished the curious children, who must have been exploring somewhere when it happened and returned to see what was going on, to a strict fifteen yards away. There they stood in a gossipy huddle. Selina heard clearly from Phyllida:

"He was kissing her when we came up. Now they'll be married!"

"With bridesmaids and things?" Janet.

"Yes. There'll be a feast."

Harriet put in importantly: "Then there'll be a baby. My cousin had a marriage feast and then there was a baby."

Little horrors! Selina tried to raise herself on one elbow to tell them so, to shame them for thinking about feasts when she had been near death. But as she did so, a swirling and a rushing caught her up again, and she lay back.

"Steady," Joel said.

But eventually she came right out of it, was able to be sat up and propped against a tree. *And be bawled out by him.*

"What in tarnation are you and the kids doing here?"

"It was a nature lesson. The frogs are very good specimens."

"But didn't any danger occur to you?"

"Of course not. The children love their big blue bathtub, naturally they wouldn't be attracted by a scummy pond like this."

"But you were."

"No, it was Ignace's cap."

"Selina, are you all right?" he demanded.

"It's an astrakhan cap. His stepfather brought it with him from Europe. Because Ignace likes his stepfather he won't say no to him, but he'd much sooner nothing at all, or perhaps a footie beanie, or a fishing tam."

"Repeat all that again. No—*don't*. You're trying to tell me, I think, that Ignace threw his cap into the pond."

"I guess so. It was there, anyway. But I think when you question Ignace he'll say he was only bending over and it fell off."

"But what in heaven inspired you to leap in after it?"

"That was a foolishness," Selina admitted.

"And that answer," said Joel of her admission, "is the understatement of the year. Why? *Why*, woman?"

"I simply saw the cap, didn't think, and jumped. I knew as soon as I hit the water how mad it all was, but it was too late. The water was flaccid, but there was still an undertow, and I found I couldn't fight against it. At first I hated the scum and the gnats and the slime, and then——"

"And then you hated the pipe?"

"I don't remember that. I only remember a pull and a swirl, then something dark and clammy and choking. After that I remember waking up and feeling your" ... she flushed ... "*seeing* your face near mine."

"I was giving you the kiss of life. For your peace of mind we are not, as the children are obviously hoping, planning a wedding feast."

"Did I take long to go through the race?" she asked.

"I only saw you after the effort," he said drily. "But thank heaven whoever originally built it made it large enough for a quick transit, and thank heaven, too, the years had not corroded the pipe so that it presented rusty edges to catch on to your clothes and hold you there."

"I wonder who did build it," Selina said dreamily.

"I don't know. But I can tell you who'll destroy it. First thing tomorrow morning Joel Grant will do so, with a stick of gelignite. Please keep your brats away."

"Yes," she said docilely.

"You, incidentally, are included."

"Yes," said Selina. After all, what else could you say to a man who had just saved your life? She would probably have recovered without the—well, kiss, but, looking back on the darkness, on the choking, on the withdrawal from that bright shore, she was not so certain.

"Thank you," she said shyly.

"You would have been a nuisance dead," he shrugged.

"How was it that you came here?" she asked curiously.

"It's my territory."

"But why *here*? I mean, the old mill isn't among your usual visiting places."

"You," he informed her, "are not a usual girl." In case she took that as a compliment, he added: "No, you're a damnfool one."

"How——" she began again.

"I was looking for you."

"You had something for me to do?"

"No, I had someone for you to see."

She glanced at him in inquiry, and he went on:

"A man. Youngish old or advanced middle-aged, take your pick. He got a lift up to Tall Tops from Tallow Wood. He's at the house now."

"And he wants to see me?"

"You and Madeleine, but Madeleine, of course, is up at the Ridge. If you feel steady enough now, I'll get you up, and we'll start the walk back. Do it slow and lazy."

"Yes."

He called to the children, and they began scampering homewards. He looked down at the cap Selina had brought with her through the race and asked: "What about this?"

"Ignace doesn't like it, and I doubt, anyway, if it will ever regain its previous glamour."

"Not like you. You've recovered."

"Glamour, too?"

"I said recovered. Now put your hand on my arm."

"I'm all right," she insisted.

145

"You stumbled just then. Don't be a fool. Besides—"

"Yes?"

"Besides, I have something to tell you that might unsteady you even more than the race. You have to hear it before we get to the house."

"Yes?" she asked again.

"The fellow who's waiting . . . look, there he is now on the verandah."

"I see." Selina's voice was faint, and Joel Grant paused and turned round to look at her to find out why.

"He—he's the man I saw down at Tallow Wood," she told him.

"Yes, I thought so. He got a lift up from there."

"Madeleine saw him, too, and reported the same as I did."

"I recall. Shabby and wistful."

"Yes." Selina glanced across again. "Yes, he is the same person."

"He is also," said Joel, and his hands tightened instinctively round Selina to give her more support, "something—someone else.

"According to him, and according to papers I naturally asked for and he was able to produce, he is your—father."

"My father!" she gasped.

"Come along," said Joel sympathetically, his arm still around her.

Selina was grateful for his support, in fact she knew she could not have done without it.

Father, she was thinking, my father. Our father.

CHAPTER ELEVEN

HALFWAY across to the verandah where the man waited, looking, Selina thought a little hysterically, rather like an anxious old dog, Selina found she could not continue without first taking stock of herself. She pretended to have to re-lace one of her canvas sneakers, entailing kneeling on the ground where she could not see those eager eyes on her.

Pretending to help her, Iron knelt as well.

"Take it easy, child," he advised.

"Am I?" she begged pitifully back. "Am I his child?"

"That's for you to decide."

"How can I? How *can* I?"

"No memory to jolt you? No flashback to the past?"

"He went soon after I was born. My mother seldom spoke about him—she was like that, she never asked anyone else to share her worries, but she did say once he had told her that the responsibility of two children was too much, especially when the second child was another girl. That's too tight." Selina winced. Joel had taken over the re-lacing and at her words he had pulled the cords very hard. If she had looked up she would have seen his tightened lips.

"Sorry." His voice was gruff. "So you wouldn't possibly remember him," he said again.

"Not possibly."

"Madeleine?"

"It would be unlikely, she would be only four. Does—does she know yet?"

"Your sister? No. I thought we would break it later."

"Later?" she queried.

"Selina, the man, if not actually old, is physically old. It must have been a great ordeal coming up here, fronting us—fronting you and Madeleine. We certainly can't send him away again."

"We couldn't, anyway, could we, if he's—"

"No." Joel said that firmly. "He will not be sent away today whatever happens. But there are a few things I would like to know. Madeleine may be able to help us. Some four-year-olds have remarkable memories. Small children register characteristics that adults often miss. Some quirk, for instance, some facial identification. Like a mole . . . or a cleft chin." He waited a moment, then:

"I think we'd better start walking again. He's still waiting."

"Yes," murmured Selina reluctantly, and he gave her a quick look.

"You feel you can see it through?"

"If—if you stay with me."

That seemed to surprise him. "Where else would I be?"

"Getting Madeleine, perhaps."

"We'll both fetch Madeleine from the Ridge later. Thank heaven she's not here now. I don't know how she'd react. You're different from your sister, Selina, you're like the trees in the valley, she is like the mill."

"But without the mill—" began Selina fairly.

"There's still an axe to do the cutting, but without the trees there's nothing. But enough of this foolish talk, we're getting nowhere. Come along now." He got up from the ground, and Selina did, too.

They walked to the verandah. There were lots of things that Selina urgently wanted to ask Joel first. How she would address the man. What she would say after she met him. She knew she could not, and would not be expected to, run forward and greet: "Father!" Then what?

"Good morning—Mr. Lockwood," she said. "I'm Selina."

"Selina," the man nodded.

Selina looked at him covertly. It had been a recognised fact that she had resembled her mother. The same rather less than average height compared to Madeleine's poppy tallness, the same calm, or promise of calm when the years cured her of youthful impetuosity.

Madeleine had not resembled her mother at all, Maddie was flamboyant, a lovely paradise bird. Because of this, the two girls, though never enlightened, had decided long ago that Madeleine was their father's girl.

"Probably," Maddie had said many times, "I can blame him for all my bad points."

But this man, this Mr. Lockwood, seemed as though he never had been flamboyant even in his green years. He was also only medium height. But ... and Selina felt an unwanted tug at her ever vulnerable heart ... he seemed gentle.

"You must be tired," she said spontaneously.

"Yes. Yes, I am rather."

"Would you like to rest? Shall I bring you some tea?"

"That would be very kind," he said.

She led him to one of Tall Tops' many bedrooms, took off the counterpane and plumped up the pillow. She had an absurd impulse to say: "Sleep, Father," absurd because she still did not know, not really, absurd because if it was true he did not deserve that name.

"I'll bring you some tea, Mr. Lockwood," she said hurriedly. She went out of the room.

She found Joel in the kitchen already boiling up a kettle.

"It's too bad," he burst out, "of all times to pick to arrive! It's you who should be lying down, not him, you've just been through an ordeal only one in a million million go through. How many days in a lifetime does anyone go through a water race?"

"How many days in a year do you find a father?"

"Is he?"

"I don't know." A biting on her lip. "I don't know."

"Then take the fellow's tray in and we'll go up to the Ridge, tell Madeleine, get her reaction and views. This is a serious matter, Selina."

"Yes, a father would be."

"Also a pseudo-father would be. Try to consider it all coolly and unemotionally. How are we to know that this man hasn't heard about you?"

"About me?"

"Oh, for heaven's sake don't be so unworldly! That you're an heiress, of course."

"In three years' time," she reminded him, "unless—"

"I think you can rule out that unless," he broke in brutally, "if you're meaning Roger. Roger won't be marrying you before the time's up."

Not knowing why she said it, Selina replied: "Someone else might."

"Yes." He answered it at once. "Someone else might and damn the money."

"You mean forget tomorrow?"

"Didn't I say that from the first?" he asked. Across the brown kitchen he looked unwaveringly at her. Straight, hard and unblinking, his eyes held hers.

"I'll take in the tea," Selina said.

But when she got to the bedroom, the man was asleep. He must have been exhausted. She stood looking down on him, the tray still in her hands. He looked even older in relaxation, more defeated, more pathetic ... more unloved. Poor fellow.

But Selina could not say: "Poor Father." She went out to the kitchen again and asked dully: "Shall we go up now to tell Maddie?"

He nodded and led the way to the car.

Madeleine was hanging drapes, and was so absorbed with her task that Selina had to tell her twice.

"Madeleine, you must listen."

"Uh-huh." Maddie had pins in her mouth.

"Father's at the house."

"What house?"

"Tall Tops."

"Whose father?"

"Oh, Maddie, listen. Our father is there."

"Our—" Madeleine stepped down from the small ladder. The pins already had scattered to the floor. "If this is your idea of a joke—"

Now Joel came in. He did it firmly. "Your sister is not joking, Madeleine, she's speaking the truth, or what we believe could be the truth."

"Father!"

"Yes."

"It couldn't be!" exclaimed Madeleine.

"But it could, and you know it. He would not be an old man, indeed he would only be what this man is, between fifty and sixty."

"I can't believe it."

"He has all the usual papers of identity. I scrutinised them closely and could find nothing wrong. He also spoke of his two daughters before I mentioned them. Spoke of them by name."

"Did he know Mother had died?"

"No. He was sorry about that."

"Sorry——?" Words failed Madeleine. She walked up and down the room trying to compose herself.

Joel left her alone for a few moments, then he questioned her as he had questioned Selina. He said:

"No memory to jolt you? No flashback to the past?"

"I was barely four when he left our mother to fend on her own. I can't remember anything about him, and I don't want to. He's not even a dim figure, only a damned figure—well, as far as I'm concerned, anyway, and I intend it to remain like that."

"I can understand your feelings, Madeleine" . . . it was still Joel . . . "but can you actually do a thing like that?"

"Actually I can," said Madeleine harshly. "Mother had to work hard physically for us for the rest of her life. She used to leave me in a kindergarten and Selina

152

in a crèche while she scrubbed or put labels on tins or something of the sort. Later, when we were too old for nursery schools and crèches, she decided to come to the bush and housekeep, find somewhere that would accept two children as well. She was still comparatively a young woman, and she had to turn round and do that because the man she unfortunately found herself landed with disliked responsibility." Madeleine's voice was rising again. She finished: "And you want me to throw my arms around him and say Father!"

"No, my dear." Joel's voice was soothing. "But I do want you to take it easy, as Selina is taking it easy."

"Then Selina can do what she likes. I'm not going down to meet him and you can tell him what you please. It's very obvious, anyhow, what he's come for. After all these years he suddenly recalls he has a family. 'Let me see,' he thinks, 'they must be rising twenty-two and twenty-six. Able to support me.'"

"Madeleine!" Joel's voice was quite stern, but Madeline still stood her ground.

"I'm not returning to Tall Tops while he's there. I'm staying here at the Ridge. Joel" . . . appealingly . . . "can't I stay here?"

"Yes. Yes, Madeleine. But I, of course, must go down to the house to watch over Selina. I have no reason to believe the fellow is anything but harmless, but I couldn't take the risk of leaving her alone in the house."

"Roger can come up to watch me," broke in Selina, and for the first time in a fiery five minutes there was silence.

"I think," said Madeleine in a more controlled voice, "it would be better for Joel to be there. After all, it's his house."

"I think so," Joel agreed, "and in case you feel left left out on a branch and unprotected, Madeleine, I'll send Roger up to Redgum."

There was something wrong here. Selina looked from Madeleine to Joel, from Joel to Madeleine, but if she saw it, they evidently didn't.

"Do you like the drapes, Sellie?" Typical of Madeleine, she had finished with the subject.

"Yes. They're nice. Maddie, you will come down some time, won't you?" Selina looked at her appealingly.

"No—oh, perhaps." Madeleine must have seen a certain look now in Joel's face, and she unwillingly agreed. She told Selina that until she did come, to send up her clothes. Roger would bring them.

Selina promised unreally . . . was all this actually happening? . . . and presently Iron Grant drove back to the house.

The days that followed were the most curious days that Selina had known in all her life. It was not the fact of this man about the house, she had always had a man, and men, about the house. It was *what* man.

She still could not think of the quiet, kindly, anxious-to-please fellow as Father, somewhere deep in her she knew she never would, but she still could not help but like him. There was an innate gentleness about him, and he had never-ending patience with children. Would a man who obviously loved children have left his own? But if he was lying, acting out a scene, why? Who had told him about them? Their location? How Selina would be . . . could be . . . an heiress in three years' time? It was all too confusing.

Selina had even made herself consider her dead mother. Could it have been possible that Mother, dear, quiet, composed, serene Mummy, had been a difficult person to live with? No, never. Then even if she had, surely two children would have stood for something. Her mother, she knew, had never had any help from her husband once he had left, never even had seen him again. It had been through her own efforts alone that the children had grown from toddlers to small girls, and after that dear Unk had held out his hand. But—Father? Never.

But in spite of all the damning evidence, Selina knew she still liked the man. He fitted into the household very easily. In no time he was taking over quite a few of Selina's chores. He always did the dishes, prepared the vegetables, made the endless cups of tea that people at a timber camp seem to need. He was appreciative of everything, too, and, seeing she had so much less of the drabber household tasks to perform, Selina concentrated on, and very much enjoyed, the cooking.

Another man apparently enjoyed it. Although the agreement in the beginning was only that Joel Grant would sleep at Tall Tops of a night, most often he was there for meals as well. Selina wondered frequently about the Ridge. Did Roger go up the mountain for meals as well as guard the house each evening? An odd arrangement that . . . and yet only she had seemed to think so. Madeleine didn't. Nor Joel. Nor had Roger when he had been asked.

Madeleine in time had consented to come down and meet Mr. Lockwood. It had been a brief encounter, but amicable enough.

"He could be worse," shrugged Madeleine afterwards, "and at least he's not uncouth."

"He's a nice man," said Selina.

"Nice? Yes. But good grief, Sellie, did you ever expect 'nice' of our father?"

"No—not really."

"I expected—if I ever gave him a thought—the extreme extrovert. A bold, overriding, ruthless character. Sort of swashbuckling in a manner. He's not at all like that."

"He's considerate," agreed Selina.

"And where does that put me?" shrugged Madeleine. "I don't take after my mother, and I'm certainly not like him. No one" ... Madeleine tilted her lovely chin ... "could ever call me considerate. No, he simply can't be my parent. He must be a ring-in, intentionally or unintentionally we don't know. So we must be on our guard, or at least you must be. I've nothing to lose, you have."

"I haven't, Maddie, and I may never have."

"Has Roger said that?" Madeleine asked sharply, and Selina looked inquiringly at her. "I meant to say," said Madeleine quickly, "just watch the things in the house, that's all. You may come back from your lessons one day and find them and him gone."

"I have lessons on the verandah. I don't leave here."

"Then when you take the brats out for nature study," impatiently.

Selina shook her head. "No, he's not a man like that," she defended. "Anyway, he comes as well."

He ... Mr. Lockwood, for want of any other name ... loved to come on the nature study rambles. He loved to go everywhere that Selina and the children went. They in their turn accepted him happily. All of them were separated by distance from their grandparents, and since the bond between children and grandparents is a sweet, intrinsic thing, he filled a strong need. One day one of them said: "Yes, Grandpa," to Mr. Lockwood, and Selina knew a deep shame. These children could accept him as Grandfather without any proof, yet she had proof but could not accept him as Father.

She tried . . . but still could not. But she still continued liking him very much.

She was supervising one morning, and Mr. Lockwood was making paper birds for the pre-class children, when the sudden sharp staccato sound came, then as suddenly went. Indeed it came and went so quickly that Selina decided she had only imagined it. Imagined, too, a vague silvery explosion. But, looking up, she saw that Ignace was alerted, too. But no one else. They were all intent on their work. Mr. Lockwood, too, had not looked up.

"What was that, Selina?" asked Ignace.

"It was so quick I couldn't tell, dear. A bird, perhaps."

"It was not a coachwhip bird," said Ignace, who had sought out such knowledge, "though it had that same sharp sound. But the mother bird does half the whip sound, so Ironbark says—"

"Mr. Grant," corrected Selina.

"And the father bird does the other half. And this was only one sound."

"Well, there's no sound now. Perhaps we imagined it."

"What's that?"

"Thinking something's there but it is not."

"Oh, but there was something, even though there isn't now. There was a sort of flash, too, even though it's gone."

"I agree," sighed Selina. "However" . . . cautiously . . . "I think, Ignace, we'd better keep it to ourselves. It still could be fantasy."

"Fantasy?" he queried.

"Imagining things."

"Oh, that again," Ignace shrugged.

An hour later Selina called: "Twelve o'clock, class. Finish what you're doing, then bring it out to me."

Mr. Lockwood helped Selina with the folding of papers, then the enclosing of them in envelopes. After they were finished Selina said she would stroll down to Tallow Wood road and put them in the mailbox to be picked up. Coming back she was met by Joel Grant. He walked up the hill beside her.

"How is the Lockwood affair progressing?" he asked.

"He's a nice man."

"So was the fellow who pulled out all the chairs for the ladies and gallantly seated them, then excused himself politely and went upstairs and pilfered their handbags."

"Oh, not you, too!"

"No, not me, too. Like you, I can't fault him. Whether that's good or not remains to be seen. Did you hear the midday news?"

"I was with the class."

"A small plane missing. Well, I'd hate to be a

grounded pilot in our wilderness."

It was not until mid-afternoon that Selina began thinking of the noise and the silvery explosion again ... then thinking of what Joel had said of a missing plane.

"Oh, no!" The possibility hit her at once. She got up from where she sat.

It took some time to find Joel, one valley sent her to another, but when she did she told him everything at once, waiting for his ridicule, but still feeling he must know.

"At what time did this happen?" he asked sharply.

"It would be around eleven."

"Did anyone else hear and comment on it?"

"No one. Only Ignace and I seemed to notice."

"Ignace?"

"Yes."

"Where is he?"

"Oh, around somewhere. Why, do you want him?"

"I want both of you," said Joel. "I want you both exactly where you were when you heard the sound and saw what you say you did."

"We were on the verandah."

"But facing where?"

"Overlooking the totem tree, but the other, the sound and the flash, I mean, would be a very long overlook."

"We'll see what Ignace says."

They found Ignace and dragged him up, unwillingly at first, for he had just been initiated into the marvels of marbles, to the verandah. But when the little boy heard the keen interest in Joel's voice, he became keen as well.

"It was a sharp noise," he said, "like a coachwhip, only it wouldn't be a coachwhip, for that takes two birds and—"

"Yes, Ignace," said Joel patiently, "but wasn't there something else as well?"

"Yes. Lightning. Only silvery lightning, not gold. Silver like in Selina's weather ruler."

"Thermometer," Selina said.

"Yes," Ignace nodded.

"And where? Where did you see this flash?"

"Over my stepfather's tree, over Svanotovit, but a long, long way over."

"I see," said Joel, and he got up.

"Do you think—" Selina asked.

"Yes, I'm afraid I do. But hell, it's such a big expanse to try to find out. Beyond a certain tree helps, but that's all it is, help."

"I know more," came in Ignace importantly. "It was over Svanotovit but on the twilight jungle side of him."

"Yes," added Selina, prompted to clearer memory now, "but not as far to the twilight jungle as the Puffing Billy clearing."

"I think I get you," nodded Joel. "We'll go down now and see if we can pinpoint the direction. You two will be a great help at least in that."

"I'll keep on helping you," said Ignace importantly. "Wherever you go, I'll show you the way."

"Oh, no, you won't, old son. Nor you, Selina." He turned sternly on her. "You do realise if I take you a part of the way with me, then send you back, *that you must go back*?"

"Yes," Selina said.

"Then we'll go at once."

They went past the totem tree, down the valley, a little left of the twilight jungle but not as far as the train clearing. Then Joel sent one of them away while he questioned the other, then brought the other back and questioned again. Both their reports tallied.

"It appears," said Joel, "that something did happen around eleven and it happened somewhere over there. Right, Ignace?"

"Yes, but a long way away."

"Selina?"

"Yes . . . but far in the distance."

"All right then, we'll go up again."

"Go up?" Then both looked at him in disappointment.

"Get some men, some provisions, some medical supplies. Alert other services. You see, it could take a long time."

"You're going—over there?" Selina waved vaguely.

"Yes."

"Can't we come with you?" Ignace tried again.

"No."

"But we showed you where."

"Yes, and I'm very grateful for that. But it's going to be hard going, probably a long, hard trek, and only experienced bushmen will be needed." Joel sighed. "Besides—"

"Besides?" It was Selina.

Joel turned so that the little boy could not hear him. "Besides, I've a pretty good idea what to expect." He half-groaned.

"You mean—at the scene of the crash?"

"Yes."

"Was there only one person aboard?"

"Only the pilot, thank heaven. But young and keen and with all the world before him," Joel said in a strained voice. But the strain was gone as he turned to Ignace again.

"You can get back and tell Cooky to rustle up some nosh, Ignace." Ignace understood that and ran eagerly off at once.

"What can I do?" asked Selina, feeling suddenly helpless and empty.

"Wait," said Joel. He paused. "And perhaps— pray."

CHAPTER TWELVE

SELINA did pray. She prayed not only for a young pilot but for a group of men who had gone to look for him. She prayed for Joel. Not because of the hazardous journey . . . more than a day's trek over torturous country, so the bushmen who had stopped behind told Selina . . . but because of another, more frightening danger that had arisen.

Fire.

The mountains up here had never known the terrors of fire like most Australian timberlands, perhaps because of the plentiful rainfall and the preponderance of watercourses. But the season had been exceptionally dry . . . last season as well. Two seasons together meant that the undergrowth became tindery, that a chance spark— To make it so much worse the danger that arose now was from no mere spark. It was a fireburst. A fireburst from a crashed plane. They had accepted that fact the next day when they saw smoke rising in the far distance, it was too thick for any passing bushfire, it was a large-scale fire, a serious fire. A big tree, perhaps, but from big trees a mountain . . . mountains . . . can begin to blaze. Very soon several mountains actually were ablaze, and in the dense dark billows of smoke they could glimpse flashes of savage red.

It all must have stemmed from something much larger than a careless match, they knew, from the sun's rays on a piece of glass, the usual scrub fire causes, and the time and the direction that Ignace and Selina had given, the reports from the aviation control, only made it all the more positive. Without any doubt there had been a tragedy in the mountains, but it seemed that the tragedy was not stopping there, that it had only just begun.

Now Selina saw a different side of Roger. Although she loved him ... yes, of course she loved him, she loved him as she always had ... she had always been aware of something somehow confined in Roger, something that stopped at certain boundaries and never permitted one step more.

But suddenly Roger was no longer only that Academy graduate, that book man, though she should have known it by the gymkhana that he had another side. The first thing he ordered were fire breaks. There always had been fire breaks, but now Roger burnt them, or directed them to be burnt, literally everywhere.

Then look-outs. They were a new idea, and Roger did not stint himself on them. Like Svanotovit, these look-outs looked out on four quarters. They comprised small landings on tall trees with a break around each, accessible by steep ladders and the platform enclosed for safety by a rail. Usually they were built a hundred feet up, they needed to be fairly high to be of any advantage, and, since Roger had rostered the men for night watching, there was a chair with a cushion, a small table, a jug of water and some biscuits.

Then Roger decreed that the moment the black, red-smudged atrocity came uncomfortably closer, all the women would be shifted down to Tallow Wood.

"No," said Selina for herself, "after all, this is to be mine one day. At least" . . . a little uncertainly for the first time in public . . . "that was the idea." She looked at Roger.

Roger said nothing.

"Not me, either," said Madeleine, "after all, you're—" She also was looking at Roger. But she became silent, too.

There were radio bulletins concerning the fire, always bad ones. The blaze now was raging on three fronts. At one front, it had extended to an attacking width of sixty-five miles.

"But that," said Roger, "would be mostly scrub. It's the small intense fronts you have to watch."

The radio bulletin also reported that a party had set out from Tall Tops to locate the missing plane, but little hope was held for the pilot if they ever located the Cessna. It also hinted that the rescuers' role was not an enviable one, not now that the fire had grown to such an extent.

At that, Selina turned the radio off.

"They shouldn't have gone," Roger said. He had been standing listening.

"They had to try."

"One life isn't worth the risking of six."

Roger was worried about many things. There were millions of dollars outlaid in softwoods in the forest. He did not want to jeopardise their wellbeing with closer firebreaks, but if he didn't, they might be lost altogether. Never the eucalypts. The gums were the only trees on earth to go through a fire, burn black, then rise stronger and more triumphant than ever.

Indeed, a fire benefited a eucalyptus valley, it burned off the trash and had no hope in penetrating the iron-hard bark. But the trees in these parts were mostly planted trees, trees suitable for veneers, for building, for ship deckings, for delicate purposes as well as tough, and such trees are destroyed for ever by fire.

There was little sleep for anyone these days. Madeleine had come down from the Ridge to live again at Tall Tops. If the fire did reach them, in spite of Roger's efforts, it should deal with Tall Tops first, being further down the valley, so there was no immediate danger in leaving the new home on the hill untended. They could all go there later when it was no use holding out here any more.

Selina in the finish gave up trying to supervise the youngsters. How could they be expected to bend over books when to the south-west that mushroom of black, red-streaked smoke grew taller and wider every moment?

Roger instructed the women in hosing. Fortunately they had plenty of water, which made the situation all the more ironical, fretted Selina, a bush fire of this size in a land of flowing water, abundant water. But between the many waters lay the thick under-growth, and the undergrowth was biscuit-dry.

The women hosed the outside of their chalets frequently. Cooky hosed the outside of his kitchen. Madeleine and Selina hosed Tall Tops in turn, never leaving it less than soaked. They even did it at night.

Something had come over Madeleine, she worked as eagerly as did Selina. She often openly wondered about it herself.

"Am I the same jet-setter?" she asked. "You could have fooled me!"

"You're wonderful, Maddie," praised Selina.

"I want to be for a wonderful person."

"I know, dear. When I look across the mountain and think of him there ..."

Madeleine gave Selina a stunned look, went to say something ... then didn't.

That night there were more flashes in the black mass to the south-west, there were lightning-like spirals of scarlet and gold. Sometimes, in spite of the valleys, they actually could see flames rising.

The radio bulletins were gloomy. The fire had spread on all fronts, the sixty-five mile scrub fire now extended almost to a hundred. Nothing had been heard of the pilot ... nor of the six-man rescue party that had left from Tall Tops. The weather, the bulletin went on, was not helping. It remained hot and dry and a wind was springing up. There was no sign of rain.

By noon, a smoke pall began at Tall Tops. It was hot, choking and very unpleasant, and Selina took the children to Joel's big blue bathtub pool, as she had often disparagingly spoken of it, though today it was not so blue, the wind already had blown across masses of charcoal and the charcoal had changed the water to an uninviting grey.

Roger had called upon all the men now, even Cooky was brought in, so that the women had to take over the cooking. Mr. Lockwood, too, was found odd jobs.

The road was still open to Tallow Wood, but not one of the women had said she wanted to leave.

When she found time, Selina sought out Mr. Lock-wood. After all, he should go, this was no concern of his.

"You'll be safe down there," she smiled to the man.

"But that's not what I want," he answered quietly. "Not safety. Please don't ask me."

"We can't make you, of course, we just thought you might wish to."

"I wish to be here." He said it so sincerely, so fervently, that Selina could only smile gently and lean forward and touch his hand.

"It's as you say, of course," she assured him.

He made himself useful in many ways. Whenever and wherever a man stood at the ready with a brush and a wet chaff bag, Mr. Lockwood stood behind him with a cup of tea, or a packet of smokes. At these times Selina wondered foolishly about Joel Grant's pipe. Had he taken it with him? And his tobacco? Did he have time to fill it? Joel, where are you, how far have you reached? Don't make it too far to get back.

It was decided that if the worst came, they would all make it to the twilight jungle, there the bushes were always wet, no fire could penetrate into that damp corridor. But to reach it you would have to pass the train clearing, its erected platform of new *oiled* wood. You would have to pass the mill. Neither were operating, of course. Puffing Billy had been taken up to the ledge. But they were still fire hazards.

"Let's only hope it doesn't come to that," Roger said.

The next morning the radio bulletin put the fire as fifty miles away from them according to Roger's interpretation of the report.

"Fifty miles! We're all right, then," Madeleine said with relief.

"Fifty miles," said Roger in a tight voice, "could be less than an hour, less than that again, given a favourable wind change."

"Favourable?"

"Favourable to the fire, unfavourable to us."

Madeleine now had taken over the telephone duty. Fortunately the wire was still intact.

At noon she called: "Roger, that American company—"

"Washington?"

"Yes. They're getting it. There's twelve women there in a dug-out. Two of them have babies."

"Hell," Roger said.

By the following morning the smoke pall became so bad it could have been night-time still. Madeleine reported that Washington was evacuating its women by means of winches, hauling its human cargoes through burning trees. There was news from Orphan Point . . . everything was a charred wilderness there. State Forest further north was an inferno.

Selina did not amuse the children now, she hosed and hosed. The only child she did keep her eye on was Ignace. His stepfather was with the fighters and he had no mother to guard him.

Around midday, Roger sought her out and told her she had better start to evacuate the women and children down to the twilight jungle.

"Do it as calmly as you can," he directed, "but then I needn't tell you that."

Selina collected the first batch, and they picked

their way between sparking undergrowth to the safety of the deep dark valley between the high gorges. Ordinarily none of them, not one woman, not one child, would willingly have remained here, it was good for a visit, but it was nice to come away from. It was too eerie, too dark. Today they went gladly. Stopped gladly.

Selina came back for another group. She did this into well into the afternoon, noting on her last trip that Cooky was back on his job again in his mess.

"Friedrich" . . . she was one of the few who called him that, but then she had known him the longest, indeed, since the first day he had arrived here . . . "why are you back?"

"Because I feel I can do much more good here, *meine Liebe*, than out there banging a wet bag. This is my place, so here I shall stay. All those men are soldiers, and an army marches on its stomach. So what does Friedrich do? He fills the stomachs, fills them well. See what I have made."

Selina looked incredulously at what he displayed. Besides his yards of Cut and Come Again, there were meat loaves, sausage rolls, pies, apple turnovers.

"You can take as much as you can down to the twilight jungle," Friedrich directed. "It will be a long and hungry night. I will take some to my army. After that you will come and do it all over again."

Selina did. She went up and down four times with goodies. Each time Cooky was absent delivering his load.

Selina would probably have kept going had she not seen Ignace. The little boy was with Mr. Lockwood and the pair of them stood side by side on the Tall Tops verandah. Selina hurried up.

"I found him waiting for you," Mr. Lockwood explained. "I was trying to work beside the men, but Mr. Peters—well, he—"

"He sent you back?" asked Selina sympathetically.

"Yes. I expect he thought I was—that is—"

"I know," soothed Selina, "but he was only doing what he thought was best. But why didn't you go down to the twilight jungle with the others? That's where they're all sheltering."

"The child," said Mr. Lockwood apologetically. "He wouldn't leave without you." He paused, embarrassed. "Neither would I."

"Oh," said Selina, embarrassed herself, "oh. We'd better go now."

It was still quite safe. The undergrowth here and there was crackling, a few trees had lit up, but it was still safe. Then suddenly the wind turned. It was uncanny to see it. You cannot see the wind, and yet—and yet Selina could have sworn she saw it, sworn she saw it turn. She saw it start racing up the valley at them.

"We haven't time," said Mr. Lockwood, seeing, too. "What do we do, then? Lower ourselves into the tanks?"

"No," said Selina positively, "that's right out. There was a case once at Bellbird Corner . . . the galvanised iron became red hot, the water boiled and—" She bit her lip. "No, it will have to be the old mill-race because the bathtub has disintegrated, something to do with its particular material. The mill-race has been blown up, but there's still some water left, and it's in a clearing." She paused. "Is there anything you'll need to take?"

That was easy for Mr. Lockwood. He said: "No. Everything I would want is here."

"Grab a few things from the kitchen all the same," directed Selina, "the small ones will get hungry." She went hurriedly ahead of Mr. Lockwood, but not to the kitchen, and not to her own room to collect a few things, essential things as any woman would. She went to Iron's room, the room he had used since he had started to live here. She took up his Philadelphia axe. She could not have said why she did it, but suddenly she could not bear to leave it behind. She locked it in its case and ran out again.

At the bottom of the steps were Mr. Lockwood and Ignace waiting for her. She took Ignace's hand, took Mr. Lockwood's, then the three of them began racing to the old mill site.

At once they were in an inferno. The wind that had turned was not wasting any time. The air was suffocating, there was a hideous crack of branches to the left and right, at times when a flame leapt ahead it flared out at them from in front. Sparks and embers fell everywhere, and if they had wanted to speak, but not one of them did, they would have had to scream to be heard above the roar of fire.

It seemed miles to the old mill-race, and yet it was actually brief enough to comprise a suitable walk for a small child. Ignace was going well, he was a tough uncomplaining youngster. But Mr. Lockwood... Several times Selina tried to slacken the pace, but Mr. Lockwood, guessing her intent, suddenly found hidden strength and started off again.

At last Selina said: "Can you do it, Mr. Lockwood? Just tell me. You look—tired." That, she thought, was a lie. The man looked at the end of everything.

"I'm all right. Please go on. We must get there some time."

"Yes." Selina led the way, and they did get there . . . at last.

The water was filthy with fall-out, and much of the grass around the scrap of pond that still remained after Joel's stick of gelignite had done its work was alight. But it was water and they went unfalteringly in. It was warm, and even when you dipped under to escape an ember there was no refreshment in it. Fortunately it was very shallow so that they could lie prone in it, in fact they could go right to the centre for better protection. And there they went and huddled. Selina wondered afterwards if she could have faced it had she known they were to huddle for twelve hours.

Night fell . . . the only way you could tell it was night was by a blacker black, a deeper red to the flying sparks from the burning trees. Ignace, for all the physical discomfort, was growing sleepy. With a little sigh, for she knew how heavy he would grow on any supporting arm in the hours to come, Selina cradled him. He looked up at her, eyes dropping as he spoke, speech blurring with exhaustion. "Goodnight, Mummy," he said. And slept.

For a while the two grown-ups did not speak, then Mr. Lockwood said: "He's lucky."

"A little boy who has lost his father and mother?"

"And found you. Someone to belong to. That's very important. That's the only thing."

There was a crash as other tree fell, and in the momentary light Selina saw the man's face, and was shocked. It was quite colourless, except around the lips. There she saw a ghastly blue.

"Are you all right?" she asked anxiously.

"No. No, my dear." Mr. Lockwood was very calm. "You see, my heart—" He looked apologetic.

"Then you shouldn't have run like you did."

"I wouldn't have run if only you had left me."

"I wouldn't do that."

"I know," he said, and tried to smile. "I want to tell you," he said hurriedly, almost as though there was not much time, "it's been wonderful. I used to dream how wonderful, but I never dreamed it would be like this."

"Like what, Mr. Lockwood?"

"No, not that. I'm not that. Not Mr. Lockwood. And I'm not your father. But I think you've always known."

"Yes, I knew." Selina wetted her cracking lips. "Can you tell me?"

"I want to. I want to before it's too late, because I don't think by the morning . . ." He smiled weakly at her again.

"My father?" Selina asked.

"He's still alive somewhere, I should say, and wherever he is, very much at the top of the ladder as always."

"Where did you know him?" she asked.

"At a project—an overseas project. I was working with him . . . no, I should say working under him. He was always so much ahead of everyone else."

"What was . . . what is he like?"

"Physically very like your sister . . . I should say that she's like him. Materially, successful. Successful as

174

to what he achieves. Successful in where he chooses
—yes, *chooses*, to go. But that will never be back
here," he added reassuringly.

"How would you know this?" she wanted to know.

"Yes, you should ask that. Why should a fellow like
me know?"

"I didn't mean it in that way," Selina said quickly.
"I—I'm so confused. Please tell me all you can."

He nodded, and told. Frequently he stopped to
catch his breath, to wet his face and lips with the vile
water.

"I've never had anyone to love," he proffered
simply. "No one has ever loved me. Yes, that's the
truth. I was reared in an orphanage, then when I met
the world, there was no one to meet me. I don't want
you to think I'm trying to make you sympathetic, for
I'm not. I simply had no one, and I wanted . . . wanted
terribly to have someone. Some people can get by
without. Some people don't care. I couldn't get by.
I cared. I yearned for someone—a wife, a child. But
it wasn't to be. Then I met Leone, and I thought—"

"Yes?" encouraged Selina.

"But your father came along, and at once . . .
well . . . Anyway, who would have looked at me after
him?"

"He married her?"

"Oh, no." A faint smile. "Even if he could have,
he wouldn't have. After he won her, he wasn't interested any more, but it didn't help, she wasn't
interested in me.

"I'll always remember that night after Leone left.
He'd been drinking. He said: 'John' . . . my name is
John . . . 'love them, then leave them, but do anything

175

but marry them. Marriage is a madness, a damnation. *I* should know. I married once, back in Australia. The first child was bad enough, but when the second came I knew it was not for me.'

"I listened ... but I could have killed him for what *he* had been given yet not loved and what *I* had not been given, so could never love.

"He got a better job soon after that, and went away. I don't know where.

"When he left, he left, too, all his things. He said : 'I'm starting anew, I don't want these mouldering mementoes any more.' There were a few photos— your mother must have sent them to him. Madeleine, your older sister, as a little girl, you as a baby. God, how I longed to gather the three of you to me !"

"But we would have been grown up by then," inserted Selina gently. "Mother would have since died."

"Yes."

"Then how did you know where to come to find us now?"

"Your mother wrote once when she left the city for the bush. I suppose she thought she'd better give him the address. For some reason ... or accident ... he had never thrown it out, it was still there. It was a remote hope that you would be here, but I grabbed at it. Already I knew I hadn't very long. I took the papers he left behind, and came out to Australia, and then to Tallow Wood. You know the rest."

"Yes, I know the rest."

They were silent for a long time. Trees kept on crashing. Embers fell and sparks flew out. The water grew warmer. The little boy stirred and Selina felt an unbearable pain in her arm.

"Let me support him a little while," said Mr. Lockwood.

"He'll be too heavy for you."

"Please."

So Selina put the child in the frail arms, and there they huddled for another four hours.

She did not know what made her suddenly look across at him, but something did. She bent quickly forward and took Ignace from him. Then she lifted his head so that it rested on a small bank of clay in the middle of the shallow leftover pond.

"Thank you," he said, but Selina knew it was not thanks for taking Ignace, for finding somewhere for his head to rest. She knew it was for—

For love. He had wanted love, he had come for love, and she had given it to him. She had never thought of him as Father, but she had liked him. Loved him in a way. How could she make him know this?

"Thank you," he whispered again weakly.

Selina bent forward. "Thank *you*," she said, "Father."

He gave a quick smile, it was so quick that she was not sure about it, but she was sure he had heard. Sure that he was pleased . . . and proud.

She found a hankie in her pocket . . . miraculous that it was still there and fresh and dry . . . and put it gently over his face. Then she held Ignace closer and waited for the dawn.

CHAPTER THIRTEEN

MORNING was late. There was so much grey pall for the sun to push through, so much obscure murk, that it was nine o'clock by Selina's wristwatch when she found out it was not night any more.

Ignace had wakened, but she had put her finger to her lips and nodded towards Mr. Lockwood, so that the little boy thought he was asleep. And, Selina thought, so he was.

But when the black lightened to grey, the grey to sickly primrose, Selina knew she could not wait any more.

"Come along, darling," she said to Ignace.

"And Grandpa?" Ignace looked back at the man.

"He's watched over you all night, I think we should let him rest now. We'll send someone down for him when we get back to the house." —The house! Would there be a house?

Always Selina would remember their return to Tall Tops. After picking up the Philadelphia axe from where she had placed it on a small clay island in the shallow pool, after glancing gently at Mr. Lockwood, after taking Ignace's hand, she started back . . . back through disaster. Disaster she would never forget.

Everywhere there was ruin. Everywhere there was black waste. There was not a blade of green grass. Not a flower. Trees either sprawled still smouldering along the ground or balanced precariously waiting to fall, and to shower their ashes.

Here and there, the way it is in the whims of a fire, something had been spared, or semi-spared. There were several trees burned dark on one side but still alive on the other side. A few trees looked as though nothing had happened at all. Your feet went deep into ashes. The ashes rose and blackened your face. At least that made Ignace laugh.

He did not laugh at his billycart, however. His stepfather had built it for him, and he had been very proud of it. Now it lay a tangled mess on the courtyard outside the housing . . . housing? . . . a courtyard burned and buckled and of no use any more. How, despaired Selina, can you explain billycarts to children? Explain all the little loved things they have collected for themselves? The small personal things? An old doll? A favourite book? A hugged-bare teddy bear?

For all the chalets had gone as well. The mill was gone. The platform to Puffing Billy had gone and the lines were twisted.

Selina detoured Ignace carefully round the charred remains of one of the camp dogs. It was Sam, the golden labrador. Everyone had loved Sam. Why hadn't he lived up to his reputation and sought water? Labradors always sought water. Then she saw *why* Sam had not done so, and put her hand to her mouth.

Sam was not anyone's dog particularly, but everyone recognised him as Cooky's. As Friedrich's.

And Selina had just seen a crumpled white cap outside a ruin that must be the kitchen. She had seen the end of an arm . . . What had Friedrich said to her? "This is my place, so here I shall stay." Foolishly

Selina wondered if he had been baking some more Cut and Come Again.

"Come on, darling," she said to Ignace, and fairly ran him to the house.

The house had not been touched. All the surrounding trees had, and The Big Feller was a sorry sight, but being a eucalypt he would recover.

Selina wondered for the first time for a long time where Maddie and Roger were. She had had too many other things to think about. She had had Joel.

Almost as if hearing her silent anxiety, the pair came out to the verandah. They were as drawn and ashen as she knew she was.

It was all over, Roger said with a resigned gesture. Well . . . bitterly . . . what was there left here to delay any fire any more? But, seriously, *it was over*. Rain had started north, and it was not localised. It should reach here in the hour.

No, in answer to Selina, he had not gone down to the twilight jungle yet to tell them to return, he and Madeleine had just come back from Redgum Ridge. At least from an outhouse on it that had escaped the fire.

"You mean the fire reached there?" asked Selina.

They gave her a dull look.

"There's nothing left," they said.

"The house . . . Iron's new house . . ."

"Gone. Everything's gone. The blaze leapt up to the ledge. All the things that Madeleine fixed up, all the new furniture, new drapes, gone. We'd raced up there to check things, then the wind changed direction, and—"

"Yes, that happened to us, too," Selina said.

"We managed to make it to a safe place, thank God, but Joel Grant's is no more."

... Is Joel Grant? Selina cried to herself.

They made a cup of tea of sorts, and while they were drinking it Selina told Roger and Madeleine about Mr. Lockwood. Then Cooky ... or so she thought.

Ignace was crying quietly on the verandah.

"Is his father—" began Madeleine.

"No, it's his billycart," said Selina. "And all the teddy bears and books and toys."

"Selina—?"

"I'm all right, but how can you explain beloved things like bears and books and billycarts to children? You see, the chalets are gone."

Roger got up. "Well, it has to be done," he said. He looked at Madeleine. "Will you help?"

It was not until they had left that Selina wondered about that. She had been absorbed in Ignace, and had seen nothing unusual in Roger turning to Madeleine until they had left. Within minutes, though, she felt she knew *why* she had been so obsessed with Ignace. It must have been some kind of sad pre-knowledge. Madeleine came to the door and beckoned Selina to the other side of the house. She whispered something.

"Oh, no!" Selina cried.

As the morning wore on they found there was nobody else to cry for. Apart from the six absent men, about whom no one still knew anything, there were only three victims, and in a way Mr. Lockwood could not be called a victim.

So there were two. Cooky. Anton Wolhar. Anton's

mate, who had beaten with a wet bag beside Anton, said that Anton had only spoken once. It had been to ask about Ignace. When assured he was safe with Selina, he had said : "Then it's all right." The mate then reported : "He worked like I've seen no man work. He was almost a machine."

Yes, thought Selina, but how do I tell a little boy?

There were other fatalities, of course. Brent's pigs and chickens. Several kittens. Sam. Down in the forest two dingoes had been caught before they could get away. Birds had fallen to the ground in the intense heat.

And Eustace . . . 'rich in corn' . . . would never keep down the rats any more. His beautiful skin remained to show them what a really fine carpet snake he had been, for the slough had not entirely burned away.

"He was lovely," the children wept . . . they were all up from the twilight jungle now . . . "worth three dollars a foot."

"Five," sobbed Michael, "with inflation."

As the homestead had the only kitchen left, the sole shelter, Selina took in the entire camp. She put as many as she could to each bedroom, then the rest overflowed to the lounge and the many verandahs.

The surprise was Maddie, Maddie who hated crowds and frankly disliked most people. She took over the meals, and the directing of the women cooking the meals, and obviously enjoyed every minute. But not when the supplies ran out, for the telephone was not functioning. The cars that had been prudently shifted to safety areas could have got through to Tallow Wood if there had been a road. But there was no road any more.

However, planes were going over continually, helicopters, estimating the position.

Roger, whose hands were full, sent Selina up to the ledge to mark out a message for help.

"Do it," he instructed, "by writing in the earth in large letters, then filling in the writing grooves with rolled white paper. Newspaper will do."

Because it would divert the children . . . she still had not told Ignace . . . Selina took them all up with her. When they got there she could hardly believe that this was their plateau, their lovely green ledge. Now it was a ruin like the rest. She wondered what had happened to the distillery, but the source of the oil would always be there, because the gums were indestructible.

"What are we going to write?" asked Michael.

"We'll say we're all right, then ask for food."

"Chocolate frogs?"

"I don't think so, Phyllida. It must be necessary food."

"Chocolate frogs are necess—what you said."

"Yes, dear, but . . . well, potatoes to begin with."

"Put chips," called someone. "I love chips."

"No, we might get timber chips," protested someone else. "Fancy eating wood!"

"Burnt wood, too."

"We'll put potatoes," said Selina firmly, and set Michael to do it.

Michael worked busily for many minutes, but presently he turned round to Selina. "I know how to spell potatoes," he said plaintively, "but I don't know where to stop."

"What do you mean, darling?"

"Potatototo—"

"Make it spuds, mate," said a voice—a voice that Selina had been waiting for. Crying inside of her for. Joel's voice.

She turned. Over the children's head she looked at him, looked at him, she knew, as if she was looking for a first wonderful time, because every time would be a first wonderful time with Joel. She knew she had always known it, but turned away from it, deliberately rejected it, because he could never feel like that with her, not Joel Grant. But now . . . now . . .

Yet what was this? She was engaged to Roger.

"You're all right?" How could anyone be so banal, she asked herself as she mouthed it.

"Yes." How could he answer her just in a word? Iron Grant was thinking.

"The men—" she began.

"All sound. The young pilot, too. He ejected himself some time before the crash. The only sad part is that the craft didn't make the ocean as he intended."

"Was it awful out there?"

"By the look of things it was not exactly hi-jinks here."

"No. Cooky went. And Mr. Lockwood. And—" She glanced at Ignace. She said softly, "He doesn't know."

"Then leave it to me. If you've finished, come back to the house."

"But the plane we're signalling—"

"It will have to return to base after it reads the message to fulfil the order. It's not as if it's a travelling shop. How is this?"

They watched and he wrote, then filled the grooves

with rolled newspaper. ALL-OK-SPUDS... He looked inquiringly at Selina for the next.

"Cheese," she supplied.

ALL-OK-SPUDS-CHEESE... Another inquiring look.

"Jam," said Selina.

"Apricot," begged Michael.

"No, plum."

"Strawberry."

ALL-OK-SPUDS-CHEESE-*HONEY* . . . "Now what else?"

Phyllida said wistfully: "Chocolate frogs?"

"That's too long, will chox do instead?"

"Yes," they all agreed, and the message in rolled newspaper was printed out in the grooved ashes. ALL-OK-SPUDS-CHEESE-HONEY-CHOX-TA.

"Will it work?" asked Ignace, enthralled.

"Like a charm, mate."

"I don't know how charms work."

"Then come and I'll tell you. I've something, any-how, to say about your stepdad."

"Anton?"

"Yes, son." Joel drew him to his side and they walked ahead.

There was one more to fit on the verandah that night, and already they were packed like sardines.

"That's something we could have asked for," said Michael, "sardines." He started inscribing: "Sir Deans."

"Not the potatoes that don't know where to stop again," laughed Joel. He wrote it down for him.

"Is that right, Miss Lockwood?" Joel asked de-liberately, and he did a copy for Selina. But when he passed it over and she read it, she sat still and frozen. He couldn't be writing this to her. No one would write something like this in a crowded room in a crowded house.

For—'I love you', he had written.

"Sardines," Michael was inscribing. "We'll need more rolled newspaper."

"Selina and I are going out to arrange about that," said Iron, and he got calmly up, put strong, calm fingers under Selina's elbow, and the next moment they were descending the steps and walking away from the house.

The pall still remained, but there were irregular tatters of sky now where the clouds had broken up, and faintly, very high up, they could see the first nervous prick of stars. The air was still heavy with smoke, it still stung the throat and nostrils, but pittosporum, guaranteed, said Iron, to penetrate from earth to outer space, came poignantly in with its scent of lemon, carnation and crumpled violet.

His fingers were still under her arm. He was guiding her downward. Down where?

"Oh, Joel," she said with joy when he stopped, for she had not checked before, "the totem tree is still here!"

She touched Anton's carvings lovingly. Then she released herself from Joel and leaned back against the trunk.

He stood in front of her, but with a hand on the trunk each side of her. She was imprisoned there.

"I told Ignace," he began.

"What did he say?"

"He cried a little. Then he asked me would his

186

mother know about it, and when I said that Anton would tell her himself he was relieved about that. I said I would build him another billycart."

"You have a lot of things to build, Joel. Barns, depositories, new mill, new mess, new chalets. Then there are the things that go in chalets. The toys and the teddy bears."

She noticed how, unlike Madeleine and Roger, he did not question her there.

"There is also," she said sympathetically, "the Ridge."

"The Ridge will not be built again."

"Not built again? But it was a marvellous house."

"I agree . . . but it was never home. *Never* home, Selina, only Tall Tops was that. It was a place of rooms, and after Madeleine had finished it, it was an elegant place of elegant rooms. But it never had been, never was, and never would have been, home. It had no corners where a little girl had sat and dreamed, no nooks where a bigger girl had sat . . . and dreamed? . . . as well. It had no old swing. No old playroom. No big grey gum continually told he could encroach no more but still nothing done about him. It wasn't *you*, Selina."

"Roger . . ." breathed Selina. She knew she had to say his name before—before—

"As soon as the road is open, Roger and Madeleine are going down to be married, as they should have been married years ago."

"I don't understand you," she faltered.

"But you must have understood a lot of things. At least you must have sensed there was something."

"A look between them," nodded Selina. "Maddie's

knowledge of Roger's capability up at the gymkhana. Joel, *could* you have beaten him that day? Won the event? Harry West said you could."

"I didn't take my special axe," he said. "On the subject of axes—"

"Your Philadelphian is safe under my bed. I forgot to return it after I came back from the mill-race."

"You took the axe there?" He looked at her incredulously.

"Yes," Selina said.

He took an imprisoning arm away as though to put it to another use. Then he must have decided to hold off.

"Yes, I would have won," he said. "I could beat the whole world" ... his voice rang not boastful but sure ... "but only for the right prize."

"Roger—" she reminded him again faintly, feeling something infinitely sweet and inevitable about to enclose her.

"He was always in love with your sister, she was always in love with him, but being two of a kind, when a dispute between them cropped up, neither would give in, and so they split up."

"Then Roger knew when he came here to work for Uncle—"

"No, he'd know nothing, it would be sheer coincidence, he'd just get the job through the usual source."

"But he'd know about me. Know my name from Maddie's name."

Drily Joel said: "Roger was doing an extra course in America when he met Madeleine, and she was between husbands, but" ... he looked sincere ... "I have a feeling she won't ever be between husbands again. Those two are made for each other, basically sound, but otherwise happily superficial. They'll stay in Sydney. Roger will take on what he always should have taken on . . . an executive job."

"Will he regret" . . . Selina gulped . . . "my money?"

"Down deep in him I don't think Roger ever really believed he would last out that long."

"Why did you persuade Uncle to make such a will?"

"I didn't. It was entirely his own idea. He didn't dislike Roger, don't think it, Selina, but he just didn't see him as your fellow. He was willing to be proved wrong, hence that three years' wait before you could marry. As a matter of interest, I was against it. If Roger waited three years, I argued, it would only prove his acquisitiveness. But Claud said it would give you time to think it over. Has it?" He looked hard at her.

"Too much time. I've only had six weeks of the three years and I've thought already."

"And the answer?"

"Forget tomorrow," she said. "That's my answer. But of course, there has to be two minds about that."

The hands had come down now. They were fitted tightly instead round Selina's waist.

"Tree husbandry is going to do itself very well," Joel Grant said, and his lips came strongly, firmly . . . everything this man did would be strong and firm . . . on her mouth.

"We'll live in *our* house," he said presently, "that house with the little girl and the old swing and the big grey gum. Talking of trees . . ." He let her go, then shinned easily up the totem's trunk and looked into the horn. "It's incredible!" he called down.

"Is there wine there? Joel, there could not be wine there. Not after all that searing heat."

"It's there. It's *there*, Selina. We'll have a fruitful year."

He came down again.

"Isn't your very name fruitfulness, oh, woman?" he said as he had said before, and his eyes were deep, dark and warm on her. His arms came tight around her. His lips came firm and strong again.

She gave herself back to him, lovingly, wholly.

"We have a start" . . . she heard him say with soft laughter between his kisses . . . "one small apple already."

"Ignace?" she asked.

"Ignace," he said.

Svantovit kept looking out on four quarters. Down from Tall Tops came the voices of Michael and Phyllida arguing how many e's to put on tomorrow's plane message for coffee.

Deep in the forest a mopoke called.

YOU'LL LOVE
Harlequin Magazine

for women who enjoy reading fascinating stories of exciting romance in exotic places

SUBSCRIBE NOW!

This is a colorful magazine especially designed and published for the readers of Harlequin novels.

Now you can receive your very own copy delivered right to your home every month throughout the year for only 75¢ an issue.

This colorful magazine is available only through Harlequin Reader Service, so enter your subscription now!

In every issue...

Here's what you'll find:

♥ a complete, full-length romantic novel...illustrated in color.

♥ exotic travel feature...an adventurous visit to a romantic faraway corner of the world.

♥ delightful recipes from around the world...to bring delectable new ideas to your table.

♥ reader's page...your chance to exchange news and views with other Harlequin readers.

♥ other features on a wide variety of interesting subjects.

Start enjoying your own copies of Harlequin magazine immediately by completing the subscription reservation form.

Not sold in stores!